Louise,
with love from
Sylvia

DREAMING IN STONE

Sylvia Hansford

For Pete and Geoffrey

Copyright © 2015 by Sylvia Hansford

All rights reserved.

ISBN: 1514608502

ISBN-13:9781514608500

All the characters in this book are fictitious, and any resemblance to actual persons, living or dead, is purely coincidental.

Chapter 1

Alison Delaney was tired of waiting for her husband. She stood up and dumped her watering can on the parched earth at the edge of the vegetable patch. Rubbing her back, she looked at the courgettes that straggled down the slope, and wondered how much more weeding and watering she needed to do. As the midday sun dispersed the morning haze, it was becoming too hot to work outside. The sultry heat prickled her skin, sent rivulets of sweat running down her body, and left her exhausted. Her green T-shirt was drenched and her hair itched beneath her sun hat.

At the top of the slope, the old house and its barn sizzled white in the sunshine, the closed shutters standing out as chocolate brown rectangles. The house would be cool and dark inside but Alison was reluctant to retreat indoors. Working in the garden calmed her, made the uncertainties and perplexities of her life smaller and more manageable. At the moment, her main worry was Brian's venture. He had set off at nine, in their old Citroen, saying he wanted to talk to the bank in Caillac about a loan. Another loan.

As soon as she heard a car spluttering up the hill, she abandoned her watering can, trowel and gardening gloves on the concrete path, and rounded the corner of the house. She arrived in time to see Brian turn the Citroen into the drive. He exchanged his sunglasses for everyday glasses and stepped out, still wearing the floppy hat that protected his bald spot, his face bronzed by sunshine and his shirt damp with sweat. Over the last few years, he had become paunchy and his face flabby.

He smiled at her and raised an eyebrow, as if expecting a rebuke. "I've got some more wine. Domaine de Chantelle."

"You should have used the money for something more useful." She watched as he carried the case of wine into the kitchen and put it down on the quarry tiles. "And did you go to the bank? You've been away for hours."

"You know what it's like in this place. Everything takes time."

Alison stepped into the kitchen and blinked. The vivid sunshine outside hardly stepped over the threshold, leaving the middle of the room dark. She turned on the electric light. The big farmhouse kitchen was lined with modern oak-fronted units, with a table in the centre. A fly buzzed around the light fitting hanging from the oak beams. The bell in the church steeple rang, a few minutes late, as usual. She took off her gardening shoes and sun hat, washed her hands in the shower room and combed her hair. Her face was flushed pink from too much sunshine and her tawny hair was lying flat, instead of curling as usual.

Brian drew a bottle of red Cahors wine from the case. "When do we open this?"

"We'll have it at lunch. I'll just do some salad." She took lettuce, tomatoes and salad onions from the fridge, washed them, laid a wooden board on the table and started chopping. His evasiveness suggested bad news. "I thought you were going to ask for a loan."

He placed the wine bottles on a shelf at the end of a kitchen unit. "I did."

"Were they helpful?"

"The girl asked me lots of questions. Got me to fill in lots of forms. And you know what it's like filling in French forms."

"Yes, but what did they say?"

He fiddled in a drawer for a corkscrew, placed a bottle of wine on the table, and opened it. "She went into the office and stayed there for ages. When she came out, she shook her head."

Alison let the kitchen knife clatter onto the board and looked up. "Was that final?"

"I asked if I could see the manager, but she said she'd spoken to him."

As she returned to shredding a lettuce and filling a bowl, she pondered the difficulty of raising the money needed to complete their project. "So what do we do?"

Brian took two glasses out of the cupboard and poured some wine. "Could you try Tim? He must be pretty well off."

She thought of her brother, who ran a software company in Bristol, and had the trappings of affluence – a big house and a boat on the Severn Estuary. Although Tim had often helped her with advice and encouragement, she doubted if he would be able, or willing, to lend money. "I don't know. They're paying for Alex to go through university and Zoe wants to go too."

"Couldn't you ask him?"

She poured some vinaigrette on the salad, and placed the bowl on the table, along with cheese and a baguette. As she sat down opposite Brian, Alison reflected she'd be glad of an opportunity to visit England. She could see both Tim and her mother, who was living on her own. She felt the familiar sensation of giving in. "We'd have to pay it back."

Brian drained his glass in two big mouthfuls. "That can wait 'til we get the *chambre d'hôte* running."

She buttered a slice of baguette and cut some cheese. "I suppose, if I go to England, I can go to see Mum as well."

"Of course."

"All right, I'll talk to Tim."

*

After a lazy lunch, Brian said he was going to change out of the grey chinos and check shirt he'd worn to visit the bank. Alison found him asleep in the biggest of the three bedrooms. As the heavy shutters were closed, the only light entered from the doorway. He lay, glasses abandoned by his side, the combination of wine and heat having proved too much. She stood in the doorway, hands on hips, and looked at him, lying plump and snoring on the pale green duvet. How much wine had he drunk? The bottles seemed to empty quickly and he could have been drinking in Caillac as well.

She shook her head and returned to the living room. It was a generous size, with natural stone on two walls and a big fireplace, with a shining copper chimney breast. That needed a lot of cleaning. A jagged crack ran down the front wall: the product of subsidence that had cost them a great deal to rectify. The sand-coloured armchairs had been bought in France, but she'd brought the red mats that lay scattered on the floor from home. They were still good, although they clashed with the red quarry tiles. There was a television in a corner which they didn't watch much. They'd found the French channels difficult to follow when they first arrived and, later, there were arguments about what to watch. She took the mats outside and banged them on the wall, as if she had a personal quarrel with them. Dust rose into the air and combined with the heat to make her cough and falter. It was too hot for such strenuous activities.

Instead, she found a glass bowl, and went to pick apricots from a broken old tree. The garden sloped down into an orchard, where the grass grew tall and ochre, full of grasshoppers which jumped at every step. She watched a small orange fritillary alight on a head of purple knapweed. Brian had delayed cutting the lawn and she wasn't strong enough to drag the mower up and down the slope. When she'd asked Steve to help, he responded by wheeling his bicycle out of the barn and setting off down the hill at a speed that made her tremble. Brian had promised to buy a tractor mower but, of course, they couldn't afford one.

As she turned and looked towards the house, she faced the back of the barn – properly a cowshed and hay barn. It formed a long stretch of stone covered with patchy rendering, under a roof that hung low along the sides. She and Brian had planned to turn it into bed and breakfast accommodation. It was nearly eighteen months since their builder, Jean-Claude Bouyssou had explained his proposals for renovation. They'd sat together round the kitchen table, with a bottle of *apéritif*, while Jean-Claude drew a plan. He pointed, with a finger yellow stained by tobacco, to show how the barn could be divided. Five bedrooms, keeping the area behind the main doors as storage space. They'd found his French hard to follow, and had emptied the bottle of *apéritif* by the time they understood. They would need an architect to draw up proper plans and submit them for approval, while the building work involved strengthening the foundations, renewing the roof, and providing water and electricity. Jean-Claude and his men had started work last March. Alison's enthusiasm had been diluted with dismay as they drove their big bulldozer over part of her front garden, smashing through a line of roses and mallows. At least they'd missed the old pine tree that cast a ragged shadow on the lawn. But they'd driven away and left the work unfinished.

*

Their arrival in St Thomas du Roc in 2005 had been precipitated by the death of Brian's father. The relationship between father and son had been difficult. At first, it had been punctuated by rows, which often concerned Brian's step-mother Val, until she left. It later dwindled through long periods of silence. Alison didn't expect Brian to be devastated when Eddie died of a heart attack, but his death proved a watershed in Brian's life. After the funeral, she accompanied Brian on a mournful visit to his childhood home in Croydon. Although he had sometimes seemed ashamed of the former council house, it was a solidly-built red-brick semi, with a garden where Eddie had laid paving and lit barbecues. Eddie had been a stout, ambling man with a loud voice, who seemed to fill the whole room. Without him the silence in the house was mournful. Brian led Alison up to his old bedroom, stood on the hessian mat in the middle of the floor and stretched his arms out, trying to touch something that wasn't there.

"I remember when I was little. My bed was against the other wall," he gestured. "This is where the shelves were, full of my books. The chest of drawers broke, so my clothes spewed out onto the floor, but I didn't care." Suddenly, he stopped, sat on the narrow bed, took off his glasses and sank his head in his hands.

Alison slipped an arm round him, concerned by his change of mood.

It was several minutes before he spoke again. "You know what really gets to me? Dad spent his whole career driving lorries. He lived in the same house for forty years, for God's sake. What a waste of a life."

When Brian had finished settling up his father's affairs, he made a decision. "I don't want my life to be like Dad's. I want to do something different."

"Like what?"

"Like having a go at writing that novel I've always dreamed about. Anyway, I'm bored of my job. I'm bored of this place. I want to sell up and go to France."

At first, going to France had seemed a dream but, little by little, a workable plan had developed. When the idea of setting up a *chambre d'hôte* emerged, Brian had seized on it with enthusiasm. He'd reckoned the sale of Eddie's house and their own would provide enough finance. The next year, they worked their way down France, starting in Brittany and looking at houses. Some were unsuitable, like a farmhouse with a huge, decrepit barn, while others cost too much. They stopped in Lot-et-Garonne, where they liked the countryside, with its limestone ridges, crowned here and there by Mediaeval villages, and separated by valleys with little streams and fertile farmland. When they found the house in St Thomas, with its barn that could be converted, they had bought it straight away.

***

It was after six when Steve rode up to the kitchen door on his bike. His jeans and t-shirt were dirty and stained with sweat, and the back of his neck was sunburnt. He dumped his rucksack on the kitchen floor, took off his cycle helmet and shook his mop of chestnut hair.

"Did you have a good day?"asked Alison, looking up from the sea bream she was gutting.

"My arms don't half ache. But André's mother gave us a good lunch."

"Does that mean you don't want dinner?" Alison smiled, because she knew the answer.

"Course I want dinner."

She put down her knife and stepped to the door to look at Steve's neck. "You'll need some cream on that."

"Don't fuss, Mum."

Steve wheeled his bike away, before returning to the house and disappearing into his bedroom. At sixteen, he was colt-like, with long legs and brown eyes reminiscent of his father's. Once the school holidays had started, he'd spent as much time as possible in his friend André Ricaud's house. This suited Alison, as his absence reduced the chance of conflict with Brian and she knew the Ricauds were responsible people. She returned to her preparations for dinner: wrapping three fish in buttered aluminium foil and placing them in the oven. Outside, she could hear the sound of the mower, as Brian finally started work on the lawn.

It was nearly seven by the time they sat round the kitchen table. Brian poured out two glasses of wine, while Alison took the fish from the cooker and set it in the middle of the table.

"I don't like fish much," said Steve. "It's got so many bones."

"It's good food," said Brian. "Don't complain."

Alison unwrapped the fish and passed one to Steve with a fish slice. "Did you spend the whole day picking peaches?"

Steve nodded. "I got given some that fell on the floor. They're in my rucksack." He set about taking the bones out of his fish.

"Do you get paid for all this?" asked Brian. He took a mouthful of wine.

Steve looked up from his plate. "No chance. Everyone helps out. André's papa was in charge, but all his relatives were there. It was fun."

"It doesn't sound much fun to me. Working without getting paid."

"You can't talk," said Steve. "You don't work at all."

"Don't talk to me like that!" said Brian, waving his fork.

"When did you last earn any money?"

"I'm still your father and I expect some respect." Brian rapped the table with the base of his fork.

Alison looked from her son to her husband, concerned by the rising tone of anger in the exchange. "He's got a point, Brian. We need a source of income."

Brian poured himself another glass of wine. "Don't worry about it now. We'll think about it when you get back."

She took a sip of wine, hesitating to return to a subject that had caused friction before. "Couldn't you apply for a job?"

"What, here, in the middle of rural France?"

"Then maybe I could. There might be somebody round here who needs a secretary with good English."

Brian wiped his mouth and gazed at her. "Don't know what your chances are. I suppose there's no harm looking."

"After I come back from England."

Brian raised his glass. "Let's drink to that."

Chapter 2

The attic (which Brian proclaimed a writer's room) had a dormer window in the western pitch of the roof. Below the window stood an office chair and an oak desk, on which was a computer surrounded by files and folders. The walls of the room were lined with shelves. The lowest ones sagged under reference books: dictionaries, atlases, and guides to the regions of France, while the remainder were crammed with an eclectic mixture of books: classics from Chaucer to Iris Murdoch, history and even fairy stories. Here and there family photographs and ornaments stood among the books. The only other furniture was a spare chair near the door.

Next morning, Brian walked round the writer's room, with a glass of Cahors wine in his hand, looking at his books. Some had been his mother's. The remainder he'd collected over time. He'd bought from charity shops at first, but later developed the habit of browsing in book shops and emerging with bags full of purchases. These he'd packed up, transported to France and arranged on the shelves, near the desk where he often sat writing and telling himself it didn't matter if he existed in an alcoholic haze, because several great writers had done likewise.

He put his glass down, sat at the desk and took out a packet of Marlboro cigarettes and a glass ashtray. Although Alison discouraged him from smoking in the house, this room was his private space and he could please himself. He lit a cigarette, booted up the computer and tried to start writing. In the evening it could be hot in the writer's room, making him sweaty and listless, but the morning was ideal, before the sun touched the window. He was comfortably dressed, in a blue polo shirt and jeans, and was keen to move on with his narrative. After all, his love of writing had encouraged him to study English and work as a copywriter. Now he had an opportunity to write, he ought to take it.

He took a copy of Evelyn Waugh's *Decline and Fall* down from a shelf and thumbed through the pages, which were covered in handwritten comments and underlining. The notes suggested a detailed study of the novel's structure, style and characterisation. It was a serious literary effort. And that was not all. The ring binders on the desk were full of notes, sketching out the plot of his novel, which was intended to be a satire, exposing the emptiness of the money-making culture of the 1980s. But he'd found writing fiction harder than he expected and stopped after a page of his fifth chapter.

Having drunk his glass of wine, Brian was about to make another attempt at finishing the chapter, when he noticed the pile of letters on the desk. Some were from tradesmen in France and others from his bank in Britain. Many of the figures were in red, accompanied by written warnings, which he ignored. He'd taken out a mortgage to pay for renovation work, but they were running out of money for daily living and some of the bills had gone unpaid. In a shamefaced gesture he hid them under a folder. They reminded him of the alarming truth about his life in France that he preferred to forget: debts were accumulating and he had no money with which to pay them.

The debts stirred an uncomfortable memory of the bookshop. He'd rented a shop round the corner of the main street of Pickhurst, the suburb of South London where they used to live, ordered stocks and employed an assistant. Customers came in, looked round, even bought a few books, but the income never covered the costs. He'd been forced to close the place down and re-mortgage his house to pay off his debts. That had been one of the worst disappointments of his life, but it hadn't been his fault. He'd been fooled by the bastard from the estate agents, who had convinced him that the shop was in a prime location, while in fact it was too far from the nearest car park. Most shoppers couldn't be bothered to walk.

The *chambre d'hôte* was a different matter. They could advertise on the internet, attract British people who wanted a quiet holiday away from it all, or travellers heading down through France to Spain. The place had plenty of potential. What he was doing was investing for the future, and what he needed was enough money to keep the family until the *chambre d'hôte* started earning. He was confident it would. Although his request for a loan had been turned down by the bank, he'd find some other way to raise the money. It was a just a matter of keeping his nerve.

He stubbed out his cigarette on the edge of the ashtray, and rose from the black swivel chair, which he'd insisted on buying for the writer's room. It took him a little time to find the bottle of wine which he'd lodged between books, to prevent Alison collecting it and taking it down to the kitchen. He poured out another glass and resumed walking round the room, seeking inspiration. After a while, he decided that he needed a biography of Margaret Thatcher. Since he didn't have a copy on his shelves, he could justify a visit to the English library in Beaumont d'Agenais.

Besides, a visit to Beaumont would be an agreeable change and gave him the chance of meeting his friend Carrie. He'd met her at a French class, run by some English ex pats, which he and Alison had joined soon after the family arrived in France. Although his enthusiasm for learning French had evaporated, he found Carrie attractive, liked the idea of renewing her acquaintance and knew she sometimes worked in the library. The idea of a change of scene appealed. Brian took his glasses off, polished them on a handkerchief, put them back on and left the writer's room. He emerged from the house into the bright light of the garden, and told Alison he was going out.

*

Brian enjoyed driving to Beaumont, because the bends over the ridge presented more of a challenge than the dull rural roads near St Thomas. In addition, Beaumont was a picturesque *bastide* village, where old streets struggled up a steep hill to Mediaeval walls and church. It attracted artists and craftspeople, as well as a community of English ex pats. He parked the car in the dusty market square and emerged into sunlight that pooled between the plane trees. The English library stood at the corner of one of the roads leading into the square. It was a dull, single storey modern building, with a few notices about courses and events peppering the wall by the door.

Inside, the room was full of blue light, filtered through blinds drawn to reduce the glare of the sun. Carrie sat a desk between the door and the window, where the light gave an ethereal sheen to her skin. She had a mass of light brown curls, which mixed with earrings like showers of coins, and wore a blouse the colour of saffron.

She greeted him with a smile, which showed off her wide lips and coral lipstick. "I haven't seen you in a while, Brian. I thought you were hibernating."

"It's nice to see you, Carrie." Brian drew up a spare chair, in anticipation of a pleasant chat. "But I think the word should be aestivating."

Carrie laughed. "I thought it was snails that did that. You're not a snail, are you?"

"And you're not a librarian. I thought you wanted to spend more time painting."

"I still do a morning a week here. It gets lonely painting. I expect you find that, being a writer. Though I suppose you've got Alison for company."

Brian sat back in his chair, laced his fingers together across his stomach, and looked at Carrie. She had a charisma that Alison lacked. "Alison spends her time gardening and cooking. Our life's a bit dull, I suppose."

Carrie shook her head, setting her earrings jangling. "You men. You're never satisfied."

Brian raised an eyebrow. "Meaning women are?"

"I suppose we're no better," Carrie sighed. "But are you looking for a book?"

Brian pushed back his chair and rose, guessing that Carrie wanted to prevent the banter becoming personal. "Have you anything on Margaret Thatcher?"

"We've got a biography. It should be on the third row of shelves on the left."

As Brian searched along the shelves, he was distracted by a book of political cartoons. There were only four aisles, but the range of books suggested the local English community had an odd collection of interests. He might have expected books about France and popular fiction, but there were books on knitting, philosophy and railways. After a while, he found the book he wanted and brought it back to the desk for Carrie to stamp.

"Could I tempt you to a cigarette break?" he asked, producing a packet of Marlboros from the pocket of his jeans.

She shook her head. "Not this time. You're a bad influence."

"Some other time, though?"

"Perhaps."

Brian left the library with the book under his arm and a smile on his face. He enjoyed Carrie's company and felt sure she liked him, although she sometimes displayed a wariness that made her seem elusive. If she was fancy free, he might have a chance of winning her friendship. It was true that he wasn't as slim as in the past, nor did he have as much hair, but he could make up for these disadvantages with his wit and experience of life.

If he had a friendship with Carrie, there was no need for Alison to know. It wouldn't hurt her. She was so absorbed in her house and garden, she might not mind him spending more time out. Alison scarcely seemed to need the stimulation and change the outside world offered, while he craved it. Spending time with Carrie would make him livelier, prevent him from becoming bored and dreary company. So Alison might even benefit. It wasn't as if he was proposing an affair, although the idea made him smile.

There had been other women in his life, but he wasn't proud of the fact. He remembered Tammy, who he'd met at a time when Alison was still grieving for their second, stillborn son. They had met on one of the occasions when his colleagues from the advertising agency had adjourned to the pub near their office in London. She was captivating: pretty, blonde and always laughing. They'd had a brief fling but he didn't think Alison had found out. He was glad about that. She remained in the background, loyal and dependable and he didn't want to lose her. He would be cautious and cunning.

***

During the few days before her visit to England, Alison picked the remaining apricots and made two batches of jam. When she realised she couldn't use the apricots still heaped in a bowl in the kitchen before she left, she checked them over, threw away a few that were beginning to rot and took the remainder to Valérie Couzineau.

From the moment they arrived in St Thomas, Alison had made an effort to talk to the neighbours. She discovered this wasn't easy, partly because of her limited French, but also because the village was declining. Perhaps dying. Some houses were empty, or only partly occupied. Their next-door neighbours were in the habit of arriving from Paris for a few weeks, only to disappear again. Some of the villagers were elderly, and although they might nod, or reply to her cheery '*Bonjour*', they seemed cautious of engaging with outsiders. It was only when Valérie, who lived across the road, gave her red grapes in return for a bowl of quinces that Alison knew she'd been accepted.

This afternoon, Alison crossed the road behind the church, standing ash-white in the sunshine. Together with its cemetery and a dusty triangle of grass, the church formed an island in St Thomas's only road. As Alison approached the Couzineau's gate, she saw Valérie sitting under a blue parasol in the garden, while a bush of bougainvillea in a wheeled pot nearby frothed with purple flowers. The Couzineau's garden was so full of flowers of different colours it resembled a stained glass window.

Valérie rose with the aid of a stick, the veins standing out on her hand as she pressed on the handle. She was in her seventies and had difficulty walking, since breaking her hip in a fall. However, she still took care over her appearance, keeping her grey hair permed and wearing a hint of red lipstick.

"Would you like some apricots?" Alison asked.

"Oh, these are lovely. There aren't any on our tree this year."

"We cut the trees back in the autumn. I hope that helps."

"Oh yes, Albert always prunes ours."

Alison reflected that Valérie's husband always seemed to be working in his garden, or in the local plum orchards. She suspected he thought her and Brian lazy.

"Come and sit in the shade," said Valérie, sitting down and patting the chair next to her. "How is Brian? When you first arrived, we saw him working on the house all the time. But not now."

Alison hesitated, wondering how to explain her husband's inconsistency. "He's writing a novel."

Valérie twitched an eyebrow. "A novel. That's interesting. But do you want to finish the work on the barn? It would be better to start during the summer."

"I hope we'll be able to start work soon," Alison said, realising that Valérie was exerting a gentle pressure, as she wanted to see the *chambre d'hôte* bringing new life to the village.

"Have you talked to the Mayor?"

"The Mayor?"

"Yes. You need to talk to the Mayor. There are restrictions on building close to the church."

"The architect prepared some plans," Alison said, reflecting that nothing seemed to have happened to the pile of paperwork that Michel Lavergne had produced. She knew the application needed to be processed by the Mairie, but couldn't imagine Brian going to talk to the Mayor himself. Brian distrusted French officials.

The women sat chatting about the weather and their gardens, until Alison ran out of subjects about which she could talk in French. She thanked Valérie and returned to her house. On her way across the triangle of grass, she stopped to look at the church and wondered whether the villagers would mind alterations to its surroundings. They claimed it dated from the twelfth century, but Brian dismissed this, pointing to the date of 1848 over the door, and arguing that only the foundations were genuinely old. Masses were only held every two months, as the priest served a group of villages.

Their own house was probably about the same age as the church. Albert had told them how old Henri Vincent used to lead his cattle to drink from a spring in what was now the front garden. He had owned fields and plum orchards in the valley but, over time, he sold both land and cattle, leaving only the house and garden for his old age. He'd been working in his garden during *la canicule* of 2003, when he collapsed and died. When Albert described Henri Vincent's life of hard physical labour and few luxuries, Alison felt sure he was making some point about the contrast with her apparently easy existence. But he didn't know the truth.

She found Brian sitting at the writer's desk in the attic, in the gloom created by partly closed shutters. He had *Decline and Fall* in his hand and a bottle of wine on the desk. "I thought you were going to finish mowing the lawn."

"It's too hot." He put his book down. "Too hot for anything."

"I've just been to see Valérie. She thinks we should be starting work on the barn again. She said something that worried me." Alison repeated what Valérie had told her.

He shook his head. "You don't need to worry about it. Lavergne was going to send our forms in. If there was a problem, they would have told us by now."

"We ought to find out what's happened."

"When you come back." Brian picked up the bottle of wine. "Do you want some wine?"

Alison shook her head and wondered whether to pursue her suggestion of talking to the Mayor. She thought of Brian's enthusiasm for the bookshop project, which had resembled a building without foundations. When the land moved underneath, the structure subsided. She dreaded that happening here in France, as they had got rid of everything they had owned in England. They'd sold Brian's father's house and their own, which had been heavily mortgaged, and as many of their possessions as possible, giving away the rest. They had nothing to return to. After a minute watching Brian reading as if he had no concerns in the world, she decided to let the matter rest. It would wait until she returned.

Chapter 3

Traffic. As Alison drove to Tim's house from Gatwick, that Friday afternoon, the traffic was at its worst, trailing along the M4 in a thick chain of cars and lorries, and the contrast with the rural roads of Lot-et-Garonne made it harder to cope with drivers who tail-gated, or switched lanes at the last moment. She remembered why she'd come to dislike England.

She hated crowds and considered it ironic that she'd spent much of her life in London. When her family had arrived in the capital from Plymouth, she'd looked out of the car window and believed, at the age of eleven, that the housing estates, shopping streets and office blocks were going to stretch for ever. She would never find her way in this muddle.

Her father, James Stelling, had been an engineer based at the Naval dockyard and moved to London to secure a promotion. He bought a house in Bromley, which was smaller than his house in Plymouth and more expensive, but regarded the move as a success. For Alison, it was the beginning of a period of unhappiness. She was mocked by the girls at her new school, for her accent and ignorance of the latest fashions, and found central London noisy and dirty when she visited museums with Tim. He had escaped by winning a place at Bristol University, where he rebelled against his father's control. It was only after a motorcycle accident had left him with a badly broken leg that Tim found a job in Bristol and settled down. Alison had reconciled herself to staying in South London but, when Brian had talked of moving to France, she welcomed the prospect.

Alison looked forward to the relative contentment of Tim's house, although she wondered about the reception she was likely to receive. She kept questioning her decision to ask for a loan, telling herself it was unfair to inflict her problems on her brother. True, Tim was a kindly older brother, who had sometimes taken her side in arguments with their father. She remembered a time when she'd pleaded for a chance to go on a school trip to Paris with her friends. Having hurried home excited, she'd waited until her father returned from work and sat down in the living room to read a newspaper. Tim was sitting at a coffee table with a science textbook, pens and a pile of paper.

James lowered his paper. "Too expensive."

"But Dad," said Tim, looking up from his homework, "you let me go."

"I expect you to have a career."

"Can't Alison have a career?"

James had fixed her with his cool grey eyes. "I expect she'll want to marry and have babies." He'd raised the newspaper, ending the argument.

Although Alison had lacked the confidence to try again, she'd been grateful for Tim's support. Maybe her life would have been different if she'd stayed in education.

However, Tim was now a family man with many claims on his time and money. His business was growing too. Although Tim hadn't seen himself as a businessman, he'd decided to set out on his own after the company he worked for had collapsed in disarray. He'd rented a back street garage with a friend and was now running a flourishing company, providing software for medium sized businesses. Despite his success, or perhaps because of it, Alison disliked playing the poor relation. She was still dithering as she turned into Tim's drive.

The house was white painted, with gables on each side of a central front door, and stood bright among trees and bushes which were damp with recent rain. A blue Renault Clio was parked on the cobblestone drive. As Alison stepped out of her car, someone opened the front door and two chocolate labradors bounded out.

Helen followed them. "Down Max, Jock! Don't mind the dogs."

"They're fine. I'm glad to see you, Helen." Alison gave her a peck on the cheek and patted the dogs' heads. Although she had dressed in a smart turquoise blouse and a brown skirt, Alison felt scruffy beside her sister-in-law. Even at home, Helen was well-groomed, with gloss lipstick and hair dyed blonde and blow-dried into shape. However, a strong jaw gave her face more character than beauty.

The front door opened into a hall with a polished wood floor and a painting of a sailing boat on one wall. A staircase rose ahead and a door on the right led to the kitchen, past a line of coat hooks, festooned with coats, hats and Tim's walking stick. As Alison stepped through the front door, her niece Zoe ran down the stairs with her mobile in her hand.

Zoe gave her aunt a perfunctory kiss. "Mum, can I borrow the Clio this evening? I've promised to meet Paula."

"I can give you a lift," replied Helen. "I'm going to my art class."

"What time will you be finishing?"

"Half nine."

Alison listened to mother and daughter negotiating. In the last two years, Zoe had changed from a sulky girl into a confident young woman. She was taller than her mother, with a shining mass of blonde hair, and looked poised, even in jeans and an FCUK top.

"I'll go and get ready. I'll see you later, Alison," said Zoe, and headed back upstairs.

"Teenagers. They always think their activities are so important, don't they?" said Helen. "Would you like coffee?"

"Thank you. I'll go and bring in my suitcase. I've got some apricot jam for you."

When Alison returned from her car with the suitcase, she found Helen standing by the coffee machine. She fetched a packet out of a cupboard full of coffees, teas and spices. The work surfaces were crowded with gadgets – the coffee machine jostled with a toaster, a food processor and a bread maker. The kitchen window gave a view of a long garden, where yellow and red dahlias stood out against dark rhododendrons. On the window sill a radio stood among pots containing parsley, chives and basil. The large wooden kitchen table was covered with piles of paper and empty mugs, one of which Alison moved to make space for her apricot jam.

"We're in our usual muddle," Helen said.

Alison wished that the muddle in her own house was more like this – busy and cheerful. She accepted a cup of coffee and sat down at the table.

"How's life with you, then? Not running your *chambre d'hôte* yet?" asked Helen, joining her. One of the dogs padded over, sat beside Helen and laid his head on her knee.

Alison sipped her coffee and decided to change the subject. "Not yet. And how about you? Is Zoe looking forward to going to Oxford?"

"She's glad her friend Jess is going up too."

As they chatted, Alison heard a car arriving. Tim opened the door to the kitchen, took off his tie and looped it over the back of a chair. The dogs rushed across the kitchen and milled around his legs, until he persuaded them to lie down. Alison stood up to give him a hug, and noticed his hair had receded, with a few streaks of grey in the brown. He'd abandoned his contact lenses for bifocals, and the lines at the corners of his eyes had deepened. Despite the pattern of freckles across the bridge of his nose, reminding her of the schoolboy, he looked older and wearier.

Tim sat at the table and loosened the top button of his blue shirt. "I'm glad you could come. It's a pity we haven't had a chance to visit you in France. I'm looking forward to hearing about your place."

"Have you got any pictures?" asked Helen.

Alison had looked out photographs but decided against bringing them, because they showed the barn as uninhabitable. "Not at the moment. Would you like some coffee, Tim?"

"That would be nice."

"It's not on the tourist route, is it?" Helen asked. "Is there anything to do?"

As Alison crossed the kitchen to the coffee machine, she wondered how to describe the charms of St Thomas. They were best described as quiet. "It's not far from the motorway but it's a good place to relax. There are lots of walks and there are boats on the Lot."

"I'm sure it's lovely," said Tim. "But I wouldn't want to be so far from the sea."

"I can live without the sea," said Alison, aware that Tim's enthusiasm for sailing would prevent him loving St Thomas. "But the renovation's proving more difficult than we thought. Costing more."

"Building projects have a habit of doing that. It cost us more than we expected to build a new garage."

Alison brought Tim a coffee, sat down and wondered how to approach the subject of a loan, considering Helen's suspicions and Tim's weariness. In the end, she opted for directness. "We could do with some help. In fact, I wondered if you could lend us some money, Tim."

"What are you living on?" asked Helen, raising a plucked eyebrow.

"We manage," said Alison, aware that she'd left Brian to deal with their financial affairs. Perhaps that had been a mistake.

"On what?"

"Savings and credit."

Tim stirred his coffee. "You can't go on like that for very long. You need a proper business plan."

Alison didn't understand Tim's business but she knew running it had changed him. It had made him more determined, as well as knowledgeable about everything from the price of postage to the stock market.

As they talked, Tim's son Alex opened the door. Alison was surprised to see him smart in a dark suit, with neatly cut hair, as she'd last seen him with gashed jeans and a hooded top. The dogs appeared from behind the table and trotted over to greet him.

"Nice to see you, Alison," Alex said, leaning down to kiss her on the cheek.

" You're looking very smart, Alex."

He grinned. "I've just been to a jobs fair."

"How did it go?" asked Helen. "I hope you wowed them with your brilliance."

"It didn't really work like that, Mum. I just talked to some electronics companies."

Alison was relieved the subject had switched from her financial problems. She felt guilty about being less than open with her brother. Although she hadn't told any lies as such, she had given the impression the project was near completion. Which it wasn't. She wondered what had happened to the habit of truthfulness she had learned as a child.

She remembered an incident when she was about six and had sat in the kitchen, looking in longing at a red biscuit tin standing on a shelf. In the end, she'd given into temptation and taken two chocolate biscuits. When her father asked if she'd taken any she'd denied it. He'd made her count the remaining ones: there were four.

"There were six," he'd replied and smacked her across both hands. "One smack for thieving and one for lying."

Her honesty had been eroded by later experience and, in particular, the influence of Brian. He was capable of deceit largely because he convinced himself those things he wanted to believe were in fact true. It was difficult to know if he was right.

As Alison watched Alex talking about his job prospects, her hopes faded that Tim would to agree to a loan. It might depend on Helen's influence. Helen was fiercely protective of her family and whilst she might include her sister-in-law, those feelings didn't extend to Brian. Alison could imagine Helen persuading Tim that the *chambre d'hôte* was Brian's project and didn't deserve support, while their own family's needs did. Worse, there was a small doubting voice in her mind that asked whether Helen might be right.

*

When Alison came downstairs the next morning, she found Tim in the kitchen with the dogs milling round him. Looking more relaxed than the previous evening, in cargo trousers and a green T-shirt, he took a tin of dog food out of the fridge, filled two bowls and put them on the floor near the back door. She looked out at the garden, noticed dew on the grass and blue tits on a bird feeder on the lawn. It was easy to feel nostalgic for English summers, with their constantly changing cloud patterns, and days at the seaside, like those she remembered from her childhood. She was growing tired of a French summer. Even when clouds billowed during the afternoon, they vanished without rain, and plants wilted and died. When Tim collected his stick and suggested a walk with the dogs, she agreed without hesitation.

After walking between houses for a while, they took a path which passed an old pub and led uphill. Alison was glad to feel a cool breeze on her face and see an open hillside ahead. It was a steady climb and Tim's limp was worsening. "Can't you do anything about your leg?"

He sighed. "I could have a knee replacement but you know how I loathe hospitals."

She remembered the evening her father had got a phone call from Tim's girlfriend Sally. They'd crashed on their motorcycling holiday in Spain. Her mother had gone white but James was angry and reluctant to give his son help to get home. When Tim returned to England with his leg in plaster he vowed never to go near a hospital again. His relationship with Sally had fizzled out, because her family blamed him for the crash. The experience had made Tim a more cautious person.

The path emerged into grassland dotted with windswept trees and gorse bushes which flamed yellow. Tim let the dogs off the leash and they bounded away. Alison watched them rushing off the path and envied their simple physical enjoyment. A moment later, she realised the hill reached a cliff and beyond, the Bristol Channel shone blue-grey. The breeze gave the water the look of being ploughed, even seen from a distance.

"You're right. We are a long way from the sea in France," she said.

"Are you set on staying there?"

Alison wondered if he was trying to persuade her to leave St Thomas. "I love the place," she insisted.

"But you need a decent income."

"We'll be all right once this *chambre d'hôte's* up and running."

He shook his head. "You'd have to earn a lot to cover your costs."

She followed one of the dogs, which was scraping at the mouth of a rabbit hole under a gorse bush. Of course, she and Brian had discussed how much the *chambre d'hôte* could earn, but in his enthusiasm, he'd underestimated the complexity and cost of the renovation work. She was beginning to wish she'd asked more questions.

"Come here, Max," shouted Tim. "They're always after rabbits." Once the dogs had returned to the path, they walked on. "You remember when I set up my company? I had to go through a long process working out markets, the costs of renting office space, cash flow, everything. It was worth it in the end. But I don't know if you've done that."

Alison stopped and watched a couple of yachts trying to tack out to sea. It took her several minutes to regain control of her growing anxiety. "I don't know what we're going to do if we can't make it work."

He sighed. "Well, I'll lend you some money to be going on with. But if you're in trouble, let me know."

"I'd be really grateful," she said and added in a rush "but we could do with several thousand."

"I can let you have ten thousand. Of course, I want it back, but I can wait."

"That's really good of you." At last Alison smiled and filled her lungs with air which carried the faint salt smell of sea.

As they approached the cliff edge, Tim clipped the dogs' leads on their collars. "We'd like to come and see your place. We both need a holiday."

"I thought you looked tired."

"That's what comes of trying to run a business. It's a lot of work. Could we come over in the autumn, once Zoe's at Oxford?"

"We'd be glad to have you."

For a while, they stood together on the headland. Below, waves were ebbing and flowing over pavements of dark rock. Alison watched the boats making slow progress out at sea, and remembered childhood sailing trips with her father and Tim. Those times seemed idyllic, compared to her present position. Her mood swung between relief and renewed worry. True, Tim's loan would help get the work under way again but it wouldn't be enough on its own. Moreover she wasn't sure how far the conversion of the barns would have progressed by the time he and Helen arrived. It had been so easy, when they started the project, to imagine herself welcoming visitors at the door of the *chambre d'hôte*. However, the renovation work had taken so long and involved so many difficulties, she'd almost lost sight of the vision. She found herself mentally crossing her fingers and hoping for the best.

Chapter 4

The gardens were large and leafy in the street in Bromley where Alison's mother lived. However, there weren't many children playing outside when Alison arrived in mid-afternoon. Perhaps they had gone on holiday, or were indoors playing computer games; perhaps the occupants of these houses were the same generation as her mother, so their children had long since grown up and moved away. The street was quiet and sad without them.

As Alison parked the hired car outside her mother's house, she noticed something had changed. The house was as she remembered, with grey stuccoed walls, a porch which her father had enclosed and roses her mother had planted as soon as they arrived. However a statue of a girl in classical drapery had appeared in the middle of the lawn. James would have banned it. He'd seen himself as more cultured than his wife, and appointed himself arbiter of taste, discouraging anything that struck him as vulgar or kitsch. He'd chosen furniture which was well-made but plain, and furnishings in shades of cream, beige and bronze. In the six years since his death, Daphne had emerged from the shadow of her husband and become increasingly confident of asserting her own views and tastes. The cats had been the first innovation but others had followed. Alison saw the statue as a good sign.

Nevertheless, she felt uneasy as she approached the house. When she and Brian had left for France, her mother insisted she was 'all right', but Daphne's phone calls were sometimes querulous. Alison imagined her growing weak and fretful with increasing age and felt a dragging guilt. Although it was unfair to accuse her of neglecting her mother when she lived in another country, there was always a case that she shouldn't have gone. Brian argued her first responsibility was to him and Steve, and Daphne would ask for help if she needed it. Alison was less sure. Her mother was not without pride.

Daphne appeared at the front door with a tabby cat at her feet. As Daphne embraced her, her arms were thinner than Alison remembered, and the flowered blouse she wore looked made for a bigger woman. At least she'd had her grey hair cut in a neat bob.

"I'm so glad to see you. It's a long time since you were here."

"I'm sorry," Alison said, and told herself not to apologise.

As she followed her mother along the dark hall, Alison noticed a little occasional table had blossomed with a collection of china animals: mainly cats and little birds. James would have thought them vulgar. In the narrow kitchen, Daphne made tea and took a packet of biscuits out of a cupboard. Apart from the biscuits, the cupboard contained only a box of tea bags, a tin of chopped tomatoes, a packet of bran flakes and several tins of cat food. Alison remembered the cupboards being packed with food in her childhood, and wondered if her mother was neglecting herself.

"Are you getting enough to eat?" she asked.

"Oh, I eat, but I please myself. I don't do much cooking. It's not worth it if you're on your own."

Alison loaded the tea and biscuits onto a tray and carried them into the living room. The brown chairs were familiar but the seats were sagging. She pushed a black and white cat gently off a chair and sat down. After a few moments, the cat jumped onto her lap.

"I'm surprised you don't have animals," Daphne said.

"Brian's not keen." On the whole, Alison was glad that Brian hadn't decided to keep goats or chickens.

"I'm glad of the company. I get lonely you know."

Alison sipped her tea, uncomfortable under these hints that Daphne thought herself abandoned. At present, there was little she could do, as she was finding it difficult enough to hold her own family together, without visiting her mother. Alison would have liked to discuss her problems with Daphne, telling her the whole truth, instead of keeping it veiled, but she was afraid of adding another set of worries to her mother's distress. She awaited the inevitable questions uneasily.

"How are you anyway?" asked Daphne.

"We're all right. Steve will be starting the second year of *lycée* in September, Brian's still writing his novel and the work on the barn ..." She fizzled out, aware that Daphne was watching her, and knew her mother's mind was as sharp as ever and she'd sensed the hesitation.

"Something's wrong, isn't it?" asked Daphne.

"We haven't got enough money to finish it, " Alison admitted, relieved to be free of the pretence.

"Brian's not sensible with money, is he? Now your Dad was different. We always managed to live on what he earned."

Alison thought of Brian's attempt to run a bookshop, recognised the truth in her mother's criticism, but sought to moderate it. "Brian's more prepared to take risks."

"Well, it's no use looking to me for money. I've enough to live on but..."

"I wasn't going to ask." Alison wasn't sure how much Daphne had to spare, and was grateful for the occasional presents she gave Steve.

"Why don't you sell up and come home? That way I'd get to

see you." There were tears in Daphne's eyes.

"Oh Mum," said Alison, getting up and wrapping her arm round her mother's thin shoulders. "You know I'd always come if you needed me."

"It's not that, really. I just miss you." Daphne dried her eyes. "You know, I've half a mind to sell this house and move into one of those homes. At least there'd be people to talk to."

A twinge of anger made Alison's voice snappy. "You'd hate a home."

"I don't know."

Alison offered to cook an evening meal and was pleased to find two chicken portions and some fresh vegetables in the fridge. The two women sat down to eat at the polished oak dining table, and talked about old and new friends. Alison's anxieties about her mother diminished as Daphne talked about the local history society she'd joined. Despite her complaints, she appeared to be keeping herself occupied, meeting new people and developing new interests.

*

In the evening, Alison climbed to the room she'd occupied in girlhood and found it full of memories. Her single bed had been replaced by a sofa, but the view from the window was almost as she remembered. She had spent hours watching birds in the oak tree at the end of the end of the garden, and her father had kept his boat in a space now covered by grass and thistles. There were two shelves, lined with books, some of which had been hers, and some family photos. She took the photos down and looked at them. One showed her with Brian and Steve in the garden of their house in Pickhurst, and she was clearly pregnant.

The pain of the memory had never left, although she had

buried it under the details of everyday life. It now returned to overwhelm her. When Steve was two, she'd realised she was pregnant again, and had been delighted. She'd applied for maternity leave from work and persuaded Brian to fetch a baby seat and clothes from the loft. Although she told everybody she didn't mind if the baby was a boy or girl, she had a secret longing for a daughter. She'd drawn up lists of girl's names and bought pink clothes.

The early scan seemed normal but Alison started to grow worried. The baby seemed to be moving less than Steve had done and, at twenty two weeks she was no longer aware of movement. She saw her doctor and he referred her to the hospital for a scan. She sat in a bleak cubicle for what seemed to be hours. Outside, buckets clanged and trolleys rattled, but the sound that was hardest to bear was women chatting about their babies. Eventually a young woman doctor came through the curtains and said Alison's baby had died. She hardly understood. Her mind had been so full of hope for the child she had been expecting. At first, she refused to listen to the doctor's advice to induce labour early, as she wanted to wait to see if there was a chance the baby was still alive. It was a while before she gave in.

Brian sat by her side throughout the labour and the pain was dulled by drugs. But nothing could lift the sense of hopelessness that lay over the whole procedure. At the end, the midwife laid a little bundle in Alison's arms. She saw the baby was a boy, said she'd call him James and didn't want to let go of him. When the midwife took him away, she collapsed in tears.

At first, Brian tried to help with Steve and housework but Alison couldn't emerge from a period of bleakness. Her distress increased when Brian started spending longer away from home. Although she realised her company was dreary, she wondered if there was an additional reason. Another woman. It was only the need to look after Steve that kept her sane. By the time she dared to think of trying for another child, Brian was working on his plans for the bookshop. The idea was postponed and postponed again, because it was never the right time for another child, until it disappeared altogether. She had long accepted that Steve was her only child but, as a result, she loved him with an intensity which she could hardly believe possible. Now he was growing up and beginning to yearn for independence, she was finding it almost impossible to let go. Part of her wanted to keep him at her side for ever.

***

Whilst Alison was away, Brian took the opportunity to visit Carrie in Beaumont. He walked up a cobbled street, which began at the square with estate agents and shops selling household goods. As he climbed, shops gave way to old stone houses, some with cast iron balconies and doorways flanked with pots full of bright red geraniums and blue lobelia. On the left, a tiny courtyard opened up, with a stone seat where a couple of old women sat. Narrow alleys beyond led to unknown destinations. Swifts screeched high up between eaves. However, patchy rendering and signs announcing in French and English *A Vendre, For Sale* suggested the picturesque surface hid real decline.

Brian was pleased with himself, because he'd managed to persuade Carrie to show him her studio. This gave him an opening. He could demonstrate an intelligent interest in art, pay her compliments, ask a few questions. As things stood, he knew little about her background beyond the fact that she was English, but had lived in France for a couple of years. She didn't wear a wedding ring but that proved little. He wanted to know more.

He stopped at a peeling door, seized the knocker shaped like a hand, rapped and waited. At last, Carrie appeared, dressed in jeans and a white shirt, with a green headscarf restraining her hair. She showed him through a narrow hallway into a high-ceilinged room. Two large windows looked out over the grey and terracotta roofs of the town and the valley beneath. An easel was placed so the bright sunshine lit a partly-completed painting of a market scene, and the canvases stacked against a wall nearby. A couple of chintz- covered armchairs and a coffee table stood in one corner and a desk in another. There was a reproduction of a Klimt painting on one wall, but the overall impression was of a room meant for work.

"I didn't know you were an art connoisseur," said Carrie, regarding him with her hands on her hips.

"I thought it would be nice to see what you're working on."

"I like painting busy scenes – markets, football matches. Anything where there's life and colour." She drew a canvas from the stack and showed him.

In the centre of the painting a group of men in short-sleeved shirts and slacks played petanque in a dusty square, while women watched and sunlight filtered through green plane leaves. "I like it. Plenty of life. But somehow, I'd imagined you painting nudes."

"Trust you to want nudes," she laughed and drew out two paintings. One featured a woman and a black cat lying on an orange bedspread. In the other a man leaned against a doorway, with a towel draped over his shoulder.

"They're good." Brian hesitated and wondered what else to say. "The hands are good. So many painters can't do hands."

A phone on the desk rang and Carrie picked it up. She spoke in confident French but he followed enough to understand she was arranging to see someone in the afternoon.

As the conversation continued, he looked round the room. A little table near the easel was cluttered with paints, crayons and sketchbooks. A vase of yellow roses and a small bronze Buddha stood on the coffee table but there was nothing else hinting at the artist's personal life. He crossed the room and sat on one of the armchairs.

Carrie put down the phone and sat opposite him.

He took out his Marlboros. "Can I offer you one?"

She shook her head. "I'm trying to give up."

"Do you mind if I do?"

"Feel free." She pushed a glass ash tray towards him.

Brian lit a cigarette, sat back in his chair and inhaled. "Did you come to France to paint, then?"

"Partly."

"So you had other reasons."

"You're being nosey." Carrie took her headscarf off and shook her hair, which rippled onto her shoulders.

"I told you why I came to France." He remembered the French course, during which all the students had been asked to say something about themselves. While he'd talked about the *chambre d'hôte* project, Carrie had described herself as a painter. That was all.

"All right. My marriage had fallen apart. I wanted a new start."

"The usual story, I suppose? Another woman," he said, aware of an opportunity.

"No. I discovered my husband was gay." She shook her head. "I've been married twice, divorced twice, I've been a single mum. I've seen it all. I've had enough of men for a while."

Brian took another puff of his cigarette, then laid it on the ash tray. Aware she was warning him off, he decided on a different tack. "I didn't know you had children."

"A son. He's twenty one and he's studying at the Sorbonne. That was one excuse for coming here." She laughed. "Though it would actually be easier for him to get to London."

That confirmed his impression she was at least forty. " I can't believe you're old enough…"

"Don't try to flatter me, Brian. I know your type."

He raised an eyebrow. "Do you?"

Carrie rose and crossed over to the stack of canvases. "Can I sell you a painting while you're here?"

"I'm afraid I can't afford them."

"I have to sell my paintings to give me enough to live on." She turned to the painting on the easel. "And I'm going to have lunch with some other local artists. We want to talk about an exhibition."

He rose, realising it was time to leave. "Well, it's nice to see you, Carrie. Let's keep in touch."

She nodded and smiled as she showed him out.

As Brian walked back down the hill, he felt deflated. Although he found Carrie charming, she'd made it clear she wanted no commitments, at least at the moment. She meant to keep him at arms' length: pleasant enough to chat to, but no more. Of course, she hadn't told him how long ago her marriage had failed. Perhaps she was just emerging from a messy divorce and her feelings were still bitter, in which case it would be clumsy of him to persist. However, the difficult times would pass and he could wait. But, in the meantime, he would call in at the Café des Voyageurs at the bottom of the hill for a pastis. There he could think about the peculiarities of women at his leisure.

Chapter 5

Steve spent the day picking peaches with his friend André Ricaud, which was more fun than staying at home. While Mum was visiting Uncle Tim in England, Dad spent most of his time upstairs in the writer's room, reading and drinking. Dad still complained about loud music, even when he was half drunk, which annoyed Steve. He either collected his notebook and camera and went out looking for wild birds and animals to sketch, or he went to the Ricaud's.

André lived on a farm near the Lot, where the flat land was covered with rows of lettuces and other salad vegetables. Orchards sloped towards the limestone ridge. Today, Steve and André were helping with the harvest in one of the orchards, where there were peach, apricot and plum trees. A minor road led to the Ricaud's farmhouse. Steve stood among the branches of a peach tree, lifting the fruit gently and cutting the stalk with sharp secateurs. André worked a few feet away, and other people were picking along the nearby lines of trees.

André was taller than Steve, broad shouldered and might have been intimidating, except his round face smiled easily. Thanks to much practice, he was quicker picking peaches. "That's five boxes I've done now."

"I'm on my fourth."

"Bet you can't finish ten in the day."

"What do I get if I can?"

41

"A go at *Assassin's Creed*." André gave a grin.

"OK."

It was hot work, climbing up and down the ladder and placing the peaches carefully in boxes, which were then loaded onto a trailer. Steve's arms ached and the sun burned the back of his neck. Occasionally, he batted away one of the wasps that buzzed among the leaves. His T-shirt, which had been white, was stained with sweat and covered with bits of twig which scratched his skin.

At twelve, when the sun was high overhead and the orchard was full of dust, André's father Georges called a halt. Everyone climbed onto the trailer and Georges towed it to the farmhouse with his tractor, while his brown and white setter trotted alongside. The Ricaud's farmhouse resembled Steve's house. It was a solid rectangular building of local limestone with a tiled roof, but bigger, with another floor of bedrooms. The tractor stopped in a tidy farmyard between the house and a stone barn, which had an overhanging roof supported by oak beams. In one corner of the overhang rows of logs were neatly stacked.

In the remaining space tables had been set up and André's mother, Murielle, was presiding over lunch. She looked severe, as she was tall and wore her hair swept back into a brown and grey fold. The table was laid with plates of ham, slabs of cheese, baskets of bread, bowls of salad, jugs of orange juice, red wine and water. Steve was glad of the chance to sit down and eat.

Georges walked past with a big jug of wine, and stopped beside Steve. He was shorter than his wife and so broad chested he seemed to be bursting out of his check shirt. His face was brown and lined, but a smile crossed it. "You've done well, young man. Your parents ought to be proud of you."

Steve beamed. It was good to be praised by Georges Ricaud, who he'd come to respect. The first time they'd met, Georges had impressed Steve by walking into the farmyard carrying a shotgun over his shoulder and followed by a dog. Georges had taken Steve and André looking for rabbits, and pointed out holes in the river bank where coypu had made burrows. From listening to Georges, Steve developed an interest in the animals that lived in the countryside. When he'd linked this to his liking for art, he developed a passion for wildlife painting.

He knew he should be grateful to the Ricauds, because life had improved once he'd started at the *lycée* and met André. It hadn't been his idea to come to France. His parents had persuaded him. Dad had told him that studying in France would improve his command of the language, widen his horizons, and be an exciting challenge. In practice, he'd found himself in a village miles away from anywhere, where there was nothing to do. Before he met André, he had to choose between cycling and listening to music. Even surfing the web was difficult because broadband internet hadn't arrived at St Thomas. Most of the villagers were elderly and there was no-one of his own age. So André had rescued him from loneliness and the Ricauds added him to the crowd of people they knew.

As Georges moved on, Steve looked at the people sitting opposite. He knew André's younger sister, Amélie, whose round face looked plumper because her bobbed brown hair hung round it. Next to her was a slim girl with dark hair, streaked with crimson that matched the colour of her T-shirt and silver heart-shaped earrings.

"So we hid them in the cupboard and the teacher couldn't find them," the dark girl said and she and Amélie giggled.

She was pretty, thought Steve, although her nose had a slight curve. He wanted to talk to her but, in this group of relatives he was at a disadvantage. André's older sister Sophie was further along the table with her husband and André's uncle sat next to Murielle.

When the laughter stopped, he took his chance. " Hallo, I'm Steve. I'm a friend of André."

For a moment, she stared at him. " Steve? That's a funny name."

André tapped him on the head. "He's English. That's why he's odd."

"All the English are odd," said the dark girl, then relented. "I'm Nathalie."

"Were you talking about *lycée*?" asked Steve.

Nathalie and Amélie started giggling again. "*Collège*," said Nathalie. "We were playing tricks on the teachers at the end of term. We've finished now."

The wine jug was being passed down the table and reached Steve. He filled his glass.

"Not too much wine, Steve," said Murielle.

Steve drank a gulp of the red wine which made him feel bolder and more adult. "I'm at the *lycée*," he said. "I'll be second year in September."

"We'll be starting there," said Nathalie.

"Maybe I'll see you."

Nathalie shrugged but Steve was encouraged. He would look for her when he returned to school.

At the end of the meal, they rode on the tractor trailer back to the lines of trees. As Steve started picking again, he tried to listen to Amélie and Nathalie chatting a few yards away, but it was difficult to pick up more than the occasional phrase. After a while, he filled another box full of ripe peaches and carried it towards the trailer. Nathalie appeared round the next line of trees, carrying a full box of peaches. It occurred to Steve that he could impress her by carrying her box as well as his own. As she came close he lifted the box from her arms with his left hand. For a moment, she was enticingly close, her skin against his, warm and smelling of peaches. He managed to walk a few yards but, as he tried to load the boxes onto the trailer, he couldn't lift them high enough and they tipped. Peaches started rolling towards the edge of the boxes and would have fallen in a pink and yellow stream if one of the other pickers hadn't seized a box with a strong hand.

"Idiot," said Nathalie.

He turned, saw her standing under the trees and reddened, embarrassed and disappointed that his attempt to please her had so miscarried. "I was only trying to help you."

For a moment she grinned, before tossing her dark hair and disappearing behind the trees.

*

At the end of the afternoon's work, Steve hadn't completed picking ten boxes of peaches, but played computer games with André nevertheless. It was six by the time he collected his bike from an outbuilding and set out on his ride home. Although the heat of the day had eased, it was a long climb from the banks of the River Lot, through plum orchards and fields of sunflowers, to the top of the ridge. By the time he cycled through the narrow streets of St Thomas, he was hungry and tired. He left his bicycle in the barn as usual and opened the kitchen door.

A smell of burning filled the air and a wisp of smoke rose from a saucepan on the gas hob. Steve crossed the kitchen in a few strides and lifted the lid on the pan. A cloud rose, making him cough. The base of the saucepan was a blackened mess of something that might have been onions. He turned the gas off and went in search of his father.

All the rooms were empty and Steve realised it would be miserable to be alone in the house. It wasn't that it was haunted; Steve didn't believe in ghosts. It was more that the house was built for a farmer's family and needed to be full of people and activity. His parents had got the plaster stripped from the walls of the living room leaving bare stones. Despite the wall hangings Mum had added, he thought the place looked like a dungeon. Murielle Ricaud, who'd studied local history, had told him a story about the house. During the war, German soldiers had burst in and hauled off Raoul, the elder brother of Henri Vincent, the former owner. Suspecting him of helping the Resistance, they'd shot him in the road. He'd been seventeen - not much older than Steve.

He walked round to the back and started to descend towards the orchard. Dad was sitting on the slope, with a bottle of wine at his side. "What're you doing?" he called.

"Admiring the view. Isn't it beautiful? I love this place." Dad raised his glass in the direction of the orchard and the valley beyond. In the distance, another ridge drew a blue line along the horizon, with a château on one of the summits.

"You left a pan on the gas."

"What?" Dad started to struggle to his feet.

"The kitchen's full of smoke." Steve seized his arm and pulled him up, none too gently.

"Oh God." He lurched towards the house.

As he reached the kitchen, Steve picked up the burnt pan and waved it under Dad's nose. "We'll have to clean this up. Mum will kill us if we leave it."

Dad stood in the doorway, one hand on the jamb to steady himself and groaned. As Steve looked at him, he realised his relationship with his father was changing. If Dad drank so much he burned the dinner, he wasn't in any position to tell Steve how to behave. Next time Dad told him off for something, he could say "At least I didn't leave a pan on the gas." It gave him a kind of power.

Chapter 6

The air was hot and sticky with moisture when Alison returned to France, making physical effort a struggle. However, Brian was cheerful and keen to go for a walk along the ridge. She knew this mood: it meant he was full of glee at some success, or confident of the prospect of success. He'd been delighted when she'd rung with the news that Tim would lend them ten thousand pounds. As he'd found a source for the rest of the finance, they'd be able to complete the renovation work.

They followed a footpath that rose between white banks, where swallowtail butterflies floated between bushes. As she paused to wipe sweat off her face, she glimpsed the familiar view of St Thomas. A group of limestone-walled houses huddled round the church, and a château standing square on a rock high above. Brian strode ahead, leaving her ambling up the steep slope. He waited once he reached shade at the summit. They walked through a wood, where the scent of honeysuckle lingered in still air, and leaves hung limp. Emerging into a glade, they sat on the grass overlooking the next valley, with its summer pattern of ochre fields, green orchards and farmhouses peaceful in the sun.

Alison pointed to a bird circling high overhead. "There's a black kite. I love the countryside here." She felt she wanted to restate her enthusiasm, after her doubts in England.

Brian smiled at her "And the weather, the wine and the food."

"It's me that cooks the food."

"It's still good." He pushed himself up from the grass. "But let's walk a bit further." They walked through orchards, where the plums were plump and showing hints of pink. Ahead, a minor road climbed up the next ridge, towards the château they could see from the garden.

"I don't envy the builders working in this weather," said Alison, "it's so oppressive."

"Jean-Claude's promised to start on Monday. But you know what they're like, they'll probably have several hours off for lunch."

She stopped as they reached the junction of the path with the road. "You're sure you can raise the rest of the money?"

"Don't worry about it. I've discovered it's easy to raise money in England and transfer it to France. The companies back home are throwing it about like confetti."

"But it will take us ages to pay it all off." She frowned.

He took her hand and squeezed it. "Don't you see, we're close to success. We'll soon have a great *chambre d'hôte*. I can just see it. We can keep it simple – buy second hand furniture for the rooms, as long as it's good. I'm sure we can provide a decent breakfast. There'll be jam from our fruit. We'll have visitors from all over Europe. With a bit of work, we'll have a great future in a beautiful place."

Alison smiled. The picture he painted was so attractive and he believed in it so whole-heartedly, it was easy to accept his judgement. Yet, as they walked together up the road towards the château, there were still concerns circling in her mind. It worried her they were borrowing yet more money, when she knew the mortgage hadn't been paid off. She didn't know how long it would take to pay back the loans, even when the *chambre d'hôte* started earning. Their success was far from certain. And it was sad that their life in France was hedged in with worries about money, when the reasons she loved the place were more spiritual – beauty, tranquillity and a sense of well being.

***

The morning had come when the builders were due to arrive. Brian strode round the garden, jingling the coins in his pocket. He stopped to talk to Alison, who was picking the flowers from the roses growing behind the barn, which would be destroyed by the building work. The project on which he'd spent so much time and money was about to get moving. It would be so good to see the *chambre d'hôte* up and running.

At last he heard the lorry rumbling up the hill. He hurried back to the house, followed by Alison, in time to see the lorry turn into the drive, loaded with scaffolding poles. Jean-Claude Bouyssou slid out of his cab, followed by his two workmen. Brian shook hands and exchanged a few comments about the weather. Jean-Claude glanced at the clouds and drew his arm across his forehead. He was short and stout and wore a leather jacket over his checked shirt, despite the heat. Sweat already stood on his swarthy skin and slicked his dark hair, giving him a greasy look.

To avoid wasting further time, Brian led the three men across to the barn, opened the wooden doors and strode inside. He turned impatiently, as Jean-Claude stopped and fumbled in his pocket. Recognising the gesture, he offered the builder one of his own Marlboros and lighter. Jean-Claude stood on the gravel until he'd lit the cigarette, then followed slowly as Harun and Marcel walked along beside the wall. Marcel, who was tall and fair, was tapping and poking at the mortar and talking to his small, dark colleague. Brian listened suspiciously.

"*Ce mortier s'écroule,*" said Harun.

Marcel nodded. *"C'est foutu."*

Jean-Claude turned to Brian and said something in French that left him bewildered. He hurried to the kitchen to ask Alison to fetch a dictionary. When she arrived, they huddled by the wall, which was over a foot thick, built of irregular limestone blocks set in mortar. Brian looked from the dictionary to the wall and understood that the mortar was rotten and needed to be replaced. More expense.

"Do we have to have it done?" asked Alison, frowning.

"Suppose so. Shit."

He looked from the walls to the concrete floor of the barn, reflecting how their money had vanished. He'd thought he knew what the project involved. Surely no-one could have predicted the extra costs that piled up at every stage. As soon as the family moved into the house, it rained and water poured through the roof. He'd asked Jean-Claude to re-tile it. Later the architect, Michel Lavergne, arrived with measuring tape and laptop. He was tall with a thin face, a circle of grey hair, a little grey beard and metal-rimmed glasses. Alison said he looked ghostly. He measured and poked, made notes and finally sat in the kitchen and assured them, in impeccable English, that there would be no problem in obtaining permission. However before he left, he pointed at the crack that ran down the living room wall, from floor to ceiling. It was subsidence, he explained and recommended building concrete walls in the cellar. Jean-Claude was happy to oblige but, by the time he'd done the concreting and tiled the barn roofs, the price they'd expected to pay for the work was increasing dramatically. Brian suspected Jean-Claude of adding extra work and inflating prices. He tried to argue, but his French had little effect.

"How much is the mortar?" Brian asked, as much to satisfy Alison as to achieve any savings.

Jean-Claude gazed at him as if he was stupid. "It's not expensive."

Brian stood by the kitchen door, watching as the men unloaded scaffolding from the lorry. With much hammering, they strung it along the front wall of the barn, like a necklace of wire. They paused from time to time to drink bottled water and wipe the sweat from their faces. The air felt warm and heavy as blankets, while clouds massed above the barns. Alison poured orange juice for everyone, while Brian walked round the barn to check it was clear of obstacles, only to hurry back to see how Jean-Claude and his men were progressing.

As he turned the corner of the house, Brian noticed a white van parked on the patch of grass behind the church. The Mayor stepped out and crossed the road. He was a wiry man with grey hair and a gaunt face, whom Brian treated with wary courtesy. Brian called Alison and they all shook hands at the kitchen door.

The civilities over, the Mayor's manner became brisker. "Are you doing some work here?"

"Come and see." Brian walked towards the barn, followed by Alison, and took the Mayor through the main door and along the building. He pointed, proud of his project and glad of a chance to display it to others. "We're going to put windows here, and walls between bedrooms there."

Jean-Claude left his men working on the scaffolding and ambled over.

The Mayor shook his head. " You should have applied for a *Permis de Construire*."

"Monsieur Lavergne looked after that," Brian said and glanced at Alison, who shrugged. He realised he hadn't heard from the architect for a couple of months. What had he done with the plans?

Harun walked past, collected a bundle of scaffolding poles from the lorry and rejoined Marcel working on the front wall.

The Mayor turned and pointed at the church steeple. "You can't do any work that changes the surroundings of the church."

There was a crash as scaffolding poles collided.

"Our changes will improve the place," Brian said. In his view the village was dowdy after years of neglect and needed investment and new life.

The Mayor gestured at the long blank wall of the barn. "You can't put windows in the front wall of the barn, or in other places that can be seen from the road."

"What?" gasped Brian. "Not at all?

"No."

Jean-Claude marched off to join his men, and the sound of hammering stopped. Brian had a panicky feeling that he was in danger of losing the argument. Frustration and anger began to churn inside him.

The Mayor waved a sinewy arm. "You can do what you like to the back wall of the barn."

"The rules seem very strict," said Alison.

"They protect the church," the Mayor said.

"Damn the church," cried Brian, the vein in his neck throbbing. His anger carried him along although he knew it was destructive. "It's not that special. Most of it's nineteenth century."

The Mayor looked at him and the lines in his forehead deepened.

"It's no good getting angry," said Alison, touching Brian's arm. "We'll just put everyone's back up." She turned towards the Mayor. "Is there anything we can do to get permission?"

"You must make the changes I've described. You can't come to the village and change the rules." With a nod to Alison, the Mayor turned and walked down the drive towards the gate.

"Fucking French bureaucrats," shouted Brian. In his fury, he took a few steps towards the Mayor before stopping, hands clenched, red faced but helpless.

Alison hurried over to talk to Jean-Claude, who stood by the barn wall with his men. The builder nodded, collected the plans from the cab of his lorry, and joined Brian on the drive.

"You want to know what we can do?" he said, and walked into the kitchen, followed by Brian and Alison. He rolled out his plans on the table. After fumbling through a muddle of things in his jacket pocket, he found a pencil. He drew black lines through most of the windows.

They stared at the plans. "That's no fucking use," said Brian.

"*C'est foutu*," said Jean-Claude.

"What do we do now?" asked Alison.

"I'll send you my bill." Jean-Claude walked out of the kitchen, towards Harun and Marcel, lounging by the barn wall. He stopped, took a packet of Gauloises out of his pocket, drew one out and lit it.

"Fuck, fuck, fuck." Brian found a bottle and glasses, sat down at the table, and poured wine for himself and Alison.

"Do you think the Mayor expects a bribe?" asked Alison.

"Maybe," said Brian, and swallowed a gulp of wine. "I'll find some way to sort this out, if it kills me."

As Brian sat at the kitchen table with his glass in hand, he knew he faced ruin. After all the work and money he'd invested. At the very time the project seemed close to success, the Mayor's intervention had stopped it dead. Finished. This petty official was about to ruin their lives, just for the sake of a mediocre church. Surely, that was ridiculous. It couldn't be allowed to happen. The Mayor was a farmer, who only understood cows, while he, Brian was a man of vision and wide experience of life. He'd ask Lavergne why he'd failed to submit the plans, and he'd check with acquaintances, to see if a bribe was required. Instead of giving in, he'd work and struggle until he succeeded. They would still realise their dream of living the good life in France. Having reached this conclusion, Brian refilled his glass, seeking inspiration, solace, or at least temporary relief from worry.

"We might as well go home," said Alison, sitting opposite him.

"What do you mean, home? This is home."

"No, I mean England."

He took his glasses off, polished them and put them back. One course of action which he was not prepared to contemplate was returning to England. Although he'd never have admitted it, he'd come to associate England with failure and disappointment. It had started at the age of twelve, when his mother had left and his father installed a step-mother, leading to rows throughout his teens. Later came the collapse of his bookshop and the end of his career in advertising. He'd finished with all that. France offered a new chance.

"At least we've got family in England. There's my Mum and Tim," said Alison.

"I'm staying here." Brian drank a gulp of wine.

"We might have to sell up and go home."

"Never." Brian thumped the table with the wine bottle. "I'm only leaving here in a bloody box."

***

Alison left Brian drinking and walked into the garden, ignoring the builders who were dismantling the scaffolding. Without thinking where she was going, she wandered down the slope into the orchard and stood among the trees. The clouds were darkening, blocking out the sun and loading the air with moisture. The countryside was waiting for rain. On an ordinary day, she would have welcomed the onset of a thunderstorm, to bring much needed water to the garden, and freshen the air. Today the coming storm only served to increase her sense of imminent disaster.

She loved the house, with its oak beams, garden full of fruit trees, and view over the valley, but she knew she was out of place here, an Englishwoman in a French village. She'd always had a private fear, which Brian mocked, that someone would find an excuse for ejecting them, like invaders or parasites. Today the fear seemed to be coming true. They might be forced to return to England.

England was her childhood home, associated with her parents, brother and school friends. But it was a dreary place, of crowded shops and traffic jams, where they'd lived in an ordinary suburban house and worked in offices. France was the place of her dreams, with its undulating hills, little villages and plum orchards, where it was a pleasure to work in the garden and walk along quiet country paths.

In any case, she couldn't return to England unless Brian was prepared to sell the house. They would have nothing to live on, and might be reduced to travelling like refugees, with the possessions they could carry. Where could they go? Her mind recoiled from the prospect of begging Tim and her mother for help. The more Alison reflected, the more she became convinced that it would be better to stay, as long as Brian was determined to do so. She would find some way to make their life in France possible.

*

It was evening when the rain began, with big drops which ricocheted off the parched earth, kicking up spurts of soil. Alison watched, concerned about Steve, who planned to cycle back from the Ricaud's farmhouse. Soon, rain poured off roofs, flowed along the concrete path around the house, and filled ruts in the front lawn, while thunder reverberated overhead. Alison knew Georges Ricaud would load Steve's bike in his van and give him a lift but she was reluctant to intrude further on their generosity. As it was, Steve spent much of his spare time at their house, and she wasn't in a position to return their hospitality.

In the end, Alison dashed for the car and drove to the Ricaud's. In a few minutes, the streets were flowing with water and she peered through the windscreen into a torrent of rain and spray. Murielle Ricaud welcomed her into the kitchen and insisted on plying her with coffee and home made cake.

The Ricaud's kitchen looked smaller than her own, because it was full of clutter. Shelves round the walls were loaded with pans and dishes of every size, while a bowl of ripe peaches stood on the kitchen table, with a fly swat beside it. While they waited for Steve, Alison sat uneasily, reluctant to get drawn into conversation about her family. Nevertheless, she was aware of Murielle's thoughtful eyes on her and started to talk about the fruit in her garden.

Steve ambled into the kitchen, scowling. "I didn't ask to be rescued, Mum."

"Do you really want to cycle home in a thunderstorm?"

His face relaxed into a smile. "P'raps not."

"All right. Put the bike in the boot and we'll be going home."

They drove home in silence. Although Alison knew they were

facing the ruin of their project, she hesitated to tell her son. The instinct to protect him from problems was still strong, but it was mixed with fear that he would judge them with adult eyes and find them wanting.

As Alison opened the kitchen door, she saw Brian still sitting, with his glasses on the table, and his head slumped on his arms. His face was flushed and his breath smelt of alcohol.

"He's drunk again," said Steve.

Aware of the contempt in his tone, Alison resorted to pleading."Look, Steve, don't be too hard on him. Everything's gone wrong."

"You wouldn't say that if I got as drunk as that."

Alison looked at her husband and realised Steve was right. She would rebuke her son if she found him drunk, because she feared that a young life could be damaged. If she'd given up rebuking Brian, was it because his problem was too great for her to tackle? Or because she no longer cared enough to try? Reluctant to answer her own question, she turned to Steve. "Help me get him to bed and make sure he's all right. Please."

Steve shrugged, but helped her carry Brian into the bedroom. Together, they lowered his body half across the bed, leaving his feet hanging down. Alison sat on the bed to remove Brian's shoes and push his feet up, then let her head slump forward so it rested in her hands.

"What's wrong, Mum?"

"The Mayor came round. He said we couldn't go on with the work to the barns. We can't put windows in the front wall. I don't see how we can go on with the *chambre d'hôte*."

"What?"

"He said it would spoil the character of the church or

something."

Steve reddened and started pacing round the bedroom. "You told me life in France was going to be great. We were going to live in this nice place and run this b&b and it was all going to be wonderful." He kicked the chest of drawers as he passed. "But I lost the friends I had in England when I came here. And I hated the *collège* at first, you know I did. And now you're telling me it's not going to happen anyway." Steve aimed several kicks at the expensive oak wardrobe. "We can't renovate the barns because the Mayor says '*non*'. So we can't run a b& b. We're fucked."

Instead of reprimanding him for swearing, Alison fished in her pocket for a handkerchief, blew her nose and wiped her eyes.

Steve kicked the door, leaving grey marks on the light blue paint, then turned and glared at her. "Could Dad get a job, d'you think?"

Alison swallowed hard. "I'll get a job. Anything. I won't let you down, Steve."

Chapter 7

In the corner of the living room stood a polished wood desk, which had belonged to Alison's father. On the wall above hung photographs of her wedding to Brian, and Steve at fifteen months, toddling across a lawn. Next morning, she opened the shutters in the living room, sat at the desk and spent several minutes looking at the wedding photograph. As a bride, she was lovely in a white lace-trimmed dress, with her hair curling over her shoulders and gleaming red in the light. Brian was smart in a grey suit, with a striped tie which looked as if belonged to an august public school but didn't. Her happy smile mocked her now. She would never have guessed, when she married Brian, that she would find herself in an old house in France, with no income. The dreams she'd had at her wedding of a happy family life were falling apart. All that was left was worry.

With a sigh, she reached up and turned the wedding photo towards the wall. She placed a writing pad by the telephone, opened the *Pages Jaunes* and the local paper. Brian had vetoed the suggestion of putting a telephone in the writer's room, as too much of a distraction. The thunderstorm had passed, giving way to a bright morning. It was very quiet in the house, with only the sound of a tractor cutting verges along the road to break the silence.

Although she'd spent the night in the spare bedroom, she knew Brian was still in bed and wouldn't surface for some time. She'd checked on him before she went to bed, eased off his outer clothes and returned his glasses. It wasn't the first occasion they hadn't shared a bedroom, let alone a bed, because Brian had drunk himself into a stupor. The kisses and caresses of their early days seemed to belong to someone else's story. Now she wondered how much of a relationship was left. Not only had passion dwindled but she no longer knew if she could trust her husband. Although she'd followed him loyally, he'd let her down. Again.

She wondered what had happened to the man with whom she'd fallen in love. They'd met at an office party in the red-brick building where she'd worked. Although it was Edwardian and grand on the outside, inside long, dark corridors ended in odd corners. The production department had taken over a conference room, Alison helped lay out bottles of wine and a barrel of beer, while a colleague rigged up a music centre with speakers.

Alison was talking to her friend Sharon, who stooped to listen, as she was tall in her high heeled shoes. A man stopped on his way to the table laden with bottles and glasses. He looked at Alison and smiled. In those days, she had a mane of russet hair, shown off by a navy blue dress with white polka dots. She'd taken care with her grooming, wearing apricot-coloured lipstick and high-heeled navy shoes.

"I'm sure I haven't met you before," he said. "I would have noticed. I'm Brian. Can I get you a drink?"

She noticed his shock of brown hair, dark eyes and sensuous lips. "I wouldn't mind another glass of white wine."

As soon as Brian left, Sharon murmured "You want to watch him. He's a terrible flirt."

Alison nodded. "Thanks for the warning."

Sharon moved away to talk to a colleague and Brian returned with two glasses of wine. "You can't have been working here long. What do you do?"

"I've been here six months. I'm Mark Danford's secretary."

"Trust him to have the prettiest secretary in the building."

"Bet you say that to all the girls," she said, smiling.

"No. Only you."

Despite Sharon's warning, Alison had enjoyed Brian's attentions. After six months working in central London, she'd felt lonely and rootless. Brian had charmed, flattered and taken her on a tour of his favourite haunts. Within a year, they were married, and she only discovered the unreliable side of his personality at their first Christmas together, when Brian came home drunk after sessions with friends of both sexes.

There had been plenty of good times, particularly their holiday near the Vendée coast, where they'd stayed in a white painted *chambre d'hôte*. Steve had fun splashing in the sea and cycling on paths through pine woods, while she and Brian enjoyed eating meals in local restaurants. That was the beginning of their love for rural France. Although the early days in their French house had been difficult, because it was cold and dirty, she and Brian had worked together to improve the place. The cracks in their relationship had grown as they started running out of money.

*

That thought shook Alison out of her memories and she turned to the *Pages Jaunes* directory to look for employment agencies. Although she suspected the jobs open to her would be the most menial, she was determined to try. To her surprise, the only number belonged to the official body that ran job centres. In England, there would have been several agencies listed. Didn't they exist in rural France?

"You speak a little French," said the woman who answered the phone, in a dismissive tone, "but can you write the language?"

"I did a course."

"You won't get an office job without good French."

Alison was taken aback by the abruptness but pressed on. "So what do you suggest?"

"Write a CV and hand it in to shops and restaurants."

After putting down the phone, Alison sat doodling and thought about the task of compiling a CV. Although she spoke French well enough to make herself understood, her knowledge of grammar was weak. In addition, what could she put in a CV? Apart from four years when Steve was small, she'd been employed all her adult life until she came to France. Here she'd worked hard to get the house and garden in order. But how could she say that to an employer? In French.

She walked up to the writer's room, turned on the computer, found a dictionary and settled to work. Although the book equipped her with words, she was uncertain about phrases, so she looked for examples, turned sentences round and tried again. Having finished writing a description of her most recent job, she decided a coffee might help. She padded downstairs to find Brian emerging from the bedroom. His hair was dishevelled, eyes red and he stumbled without spectacles.

"I can't find my bloody glasses."

"Probably under the bed," Alison said and turned towards the kitchen.

"I can't see what I'm doing."

"Are you expecting me to look?"

"Please."

She sighed and marched to the bedroom. Having collected the sheets and duvet from the floor, she retrieved the spectacles and returned them to Brian, who had slumped at the kitchen table.

"I could do with a coffee."

She folded her arms and considered him. "You look terrible."

He grunted.

"I'll get coffee but then I'm going back upstairs. I'm applying for jobs."

"Bloody hell. I can't deal with that now."

As Alison looked at him, she felt a rising sense of disgust. It hadn't mattered, when they married, that he was eight years older than her but time and too much drink had aged him. Now he was paunchy and red-faced, the sensuous lips flabby. She was angry with herself for having supported, encouraged and advised him over the years. Maybe she should have learnt from the bookshop fiasco. She sighed and wondered whether her father had taught her too well to rely on men. However she was angrier with Brian and determined that, this time, she would break with her habit of accepting his judgement. She would find a job, not just to earn some money, but to give her independence. This time, she'd take the decisions. The idea that she would be the one with money and the power that went with it was alarming but exciting. Perhaps she could build a future that reflected her own ideas and values. She turned away from Brian and shut the door.

*

Caillac shimmered in sunshine and the Lot shone like a mirror between its banks as Alison drove across the old bridge. She stopped in a car park close to the bridge and considered where to go next in her search for jobs. The town straggled around the base of a line of limestone cliffs on the north bank and spilled into suburbs across the river. She had started the previous morning on the south bank and handed her CV to two supermarkets and a pharmacy with no success. Now she intended to try the town centre. It was two thirty in the afternoon, as she'd allowed herself a morning gardening and a leisurely lunch. The small shops would take time to reopen. She'd thought about her appearance: neat but not dressy, so she chose a white blouse and black slacks, with a black handbag big enough to hold an envelope full of papers.

A footpath shaded by plane trees ran between the car park and the river. Alison followed it, passing several white boats moored along the bank, and climbed a set of stone steps at the end of the bridge. From here, she turned right and crossed the road that ran along the north bank, to reach the main street into the centre of the town. At first, the buildings she passed were discouraging, with peeling rendering and closed shutters. A pizzeria stood empty, its windows whitewashed and remnants of an awning drooping. Some doorways bore the names of businesses but no other sign of activity.

As the road climbed and swung to the right, the town took on a busier appearance. Alison hesitated outside a hairdressers, watching an assistant combing the hair of an elderly client. She decided she lacked the skills for this work. A *patisserie* nearby looked more promising, as she understood the making of the fruit tarts and éclairs in the window. She wandered in and waited, as two plump women with baguettes in their shopping bags chatted to the manageress. Alison tried to assess the woman behind the counter. The result was not encouraging: a thin face and curls that looked as if she'd just come from the hairdressers down the road. There appeared to be no assistants.

Having taken her CV from her bag, Alison held it out. "I wondered if you had any jobs here?"

The manageress stared at her for a moment. " I'm sorry but no."

From the *patisserie*, Alison continued her walk up the main street, staring in windows, passing banks and estate agents. At a newsagent, she walked in and looked at the rows of magazines and newspapers, telling herself she could understand at least the headlines. Some of the women's magazines she might be able to read, although *Le Monde* would defeat her. The man behind the counter smiled, showing white teeth under a dark moustache, as she approached. The smile vanished as she posed her question.

"Have you worked in a shop, Madame?" he asked.

"I was a secretary and I'm used to meeting people. And I speak English well."

He shook his head.

After a while, Alison reached the central square, where the Mairie and a Mediaeval church stood raised above the surrounding buildings on an outcrop of rock. Beyond, the road forked and she followed both branches in turn. After a while, shops were replaced by suburban houses with gardens. She returned, discouraged, crossed the main road and started dawdling down the other side. Although she tried offering her CV in several shops and a café, she had no success. Her feet were hurting in her smart black shoes and the heat of the afternoon left her exhausted. It would be good to sit down and relax.

By the time Alison reached the bottom of the hill, she'd decided to abandon job hunting until another day. Although she told herself there must be someone who had a job she could do, her hopes were dwindling. She thought of the Intermarché where she'd handed in her CV. The assistant had promised to hand it in to a manager, so perhaps someone would be in touch with her. Maybe she should try the bigger town of Castelnau-sur-Lot.

On the far side of the road along the river bank was a parade of small shops, including a florist, a *boulangerie* and a restaurant. From where Alison stood, Le Pont restaurant looked unprepossessing: two former terraced houses with grey rendering and blue shutters. To the left, the bridge crossed the River Lot. However, Alison remembered eating in the restaurant with Brian, on a balcony overlooking the river. That had been in their early days in France, before they decided that meals out were a waste of money. She decided to go in, treat herself to a coffee and hand in her CV.

Chapter 8

It was nearly four and the bar was occupied by a scattering of men hunched over their drinks. Alison stepped in and stood for a moment, letting her eyes become accustomed to shade. A couple of old men looked up from their drinks and stared at her. She sat at a table and looked around: white painted walls, dotted with bright posters of local events, glass-topped tables and cane chairs. It was pleasantly cool after the heat of the town. There was a well-stocked bar at one side and, at the other, an arch into the restaurant.

The young woman who took her order for a *café au lait* was plump with dyed blonde hair. When she returned with the coffee, Alison took her chance and held out her CV. "Do you have any work here?"

The woman stared at her for a disconcertingly long time. "I think *le patron* needs someone to wash up."

"Will you take my CV ?"

"I'll go and tell *le patron*, if you like. But it's dirty work."

"Please," said Alison, determined not to be put off.

Once the woman had left, Alison sat and sipped her coffee, trying to appear calm. But her body ached with fatigue and worry, and she crossed and recrossed her legs under the table. In England, she might have had decent job prospects, as her collection of O levels and secretarial qualifications counted for something. Here, it looked as if the only job she could find was washing up in a restaurant. She would take it. It was better than nothing.

The woman returned from the kitchens, took a bottle of Pernod to another customer, then crossed to Alison's table. "*Le patron* will talk to you, if you go round the back of the restaurant and knock on the kitchen door."

Alison thanked her and paid for the coffee. Outside, she hesitated. How did she get to the kitchen door? Then she remembered there was a driveway which sloped down from the bridge to the rear of the shops. She threaded her way along the river bank, between moored boats and flower beds. As she saw a large balcony projecting towards the river, she recognised the restaurant. Beneath was a patio surrounded by planters full of bright geraniums and marigolds, and six metal tables outside a white door. Alison hesitated. She took a comb out of her handbag, ran it through her hair and took a deep breath to still the flurry of nervousness. At last she knocked on the door.

It was opened by a tall, angular man, with short, dark hair and an aquiline nose. Despite the old jeans and T-shirt, she guessed this was *le patron*.

He looked at her, head tilted to one side, then smiled. "Madame Delaney? I'm François Allombert. *Entrez*." His smile was attractive, lighting severe features with good humour.

He admitted her into a hall, with white plastered walls and worn flagstones, which led to a stone staircase. On one side were two doors marked *privé*, on the other a glimpse of the kitchen. White walls and stainless steel. François opened one of the doors and ushered her into a small office jammed full of grey filing cabinets and a wooden desk. Alison noticed a photograph of a young boy and girl on the desk.

François offered her a wooden chair which was so chipped and scuffed, it looked as if someone had thrown it against a wall. "I only want someone to wash up." He seemed almost apologetic.

Alison nodded. " I know that."

"Why does an English lady like you want to work in my kitchen?"

She hesitated and realised that only the truth made sense. "I need the money."

He shook his head. "We work hard here, and for not much money."

"I'm not afraid of hard work."

"But have you worked in a restaurant kitchen before?"

For a moment, Alison thought that she was going to be turned down for even this lowly job, and found herself gabbling. "At home, I do all the cooking and the housework and most of the gardening and some of the decorating."

François raised an eyebrow. "Are you married?"

"Yes, but..." She hesitated, and wondered what this man would think of Brian. "I do most of the work."

"We work long hours," he explained. "I want someone who can start at ten and stay until late. With a break from three until five. Can you do that?"

Alison hesitated. In a swirl of thought, she worried about the effect hard work and late hours would have on her home life. How would Steve and Brian cope without her cooking? Would she find time to work in her garden? Would she be so exhausted she could do nothing else? Then cold anger took over. Brian's rashness had placed her in this position, so he should share the consequences. He could cook the dinner and do some of the housework. She would prove she was able and willing to work, even if he wasn't.

Aware that François was watching her with interest, she nodded. "OK."

At last, he smiled. "*Eh bien*. I'll give you the job. Can you start on Saturday? We're always busy on Saturdays."

"Could you show me the things I need to use?" asked Alison, struggling between relief and anxiety.

As François led her out of the office, a young girl ran down the stairs, stopped and looked at Alison. He put his hand on the girl's shoulder. "This is my daughter, Nathalie. Alison has come to do washing up for us."

Nathalie pushed back her dark hair, streaked with red and revealed gold stud earrings. "Good luck" she said, laughed and bolted out of the restaurant door.

François shrugged. "She's a bit wild sometimes."

Alison nodded, concealing a sense of unease at Nathalie's response. "Teenagers can be like that."

She followed as François stepped into the kitchen. A stainless steel sink, together with its draining boards, occupied the wall under the window. A large dishwasher hummed under the work surface. Alison looked out at a view of the river and a line of white boats.

"There's a good view from the dining room above, " he said, standing beside her. "That's why I chose this restaurant." He turned to the preparation table, which ran the whole length of the room. "There is room for four chefs."

He touched the stainless steel, and gestured towards the chopping boards, knife blocks and utensils on hooks. Above, rows of gleaming pans were stacked on shelves. With evident pride, he opened the large walk-in refrigerator, where a side of beef hung on a hook and plucked ducks occupied a shelf. Next, he showed Alison the modern ovens and a lift which took food to the restaurant upstairs. There was a pervading scent of olive oil and garlic but the kitchen was clean and neat. Alison wondered how much of the task of keeping it clean would fall to her. It would mean a great deal of work.

"If you do well, you could do simple preparation," François said.

"I will try."

Alison returned along the hall to the door, arguing with herself. In one part of her mind, used to accepting the verdict of the men in her life, there was fear that this job might destroy her home life. In another part, where the new Alison was developing, there was a sense of a new start. Washing up in a restaurant kitchen might be the lowliest of jobs but it would be a change, almost an adventure. And she had a feeling that François was a man she could work for. As she stood by his side at the kitchen door, he turned to her and smiled and she smiled back.

***

For a couple of days, Brian had existed in a state of confusion. Even after he emerged from a hangover that felt as if his skull was cracking, he'd taken little interest in Alison's attempts to write a CV. He only realised she was determined when she set off on a second attempt to look for jobs. Her initiative left him feeling shamed, aware of his own failure to act. It almost threatened his manhood. Brian told himself it was old-fashioned to insist that the husband should be the breadwinner, but the idea that Alison might be working, while he wasn't, presented a threat to his self-esteem. He needed to act.

He filled a glass with wine, and climbed the stairs to the writer's room. Having found a French dictionary, he sat at the desk and booted up the computer. He would write a strong letter to Michel Lavergne, demanding an explanation for his failure to submit the plans. First, he lit a cigarette, lent back and inhaled deeply. Thus calmed, he leafed through the papers on the desk, looking for the architect's address. He picked up Lavergne's latest bill and sat looking at it for several minutes. The realisation dawned that he'd left it unpaid.

The thought whispered in his mind that the failure of the project was his fault. Of course, it was unreasonable of Lavergne to abandon the work, rather than phoning or writing. Were there more letters? He scrabbled among papers. An Englishman like himself couldn't be expected to know the planning process was incomplete, because the rules were so complicated even the French didn't understand them. Damn French bureaucracy. Nevertheless, there was an uncomfortable feeling in his stomach as he checked his bank account to see if he could raise the money to pay the architect. Of course, there were the ten thousand pounds Alison's brother had lent them. That would cover a few bills. Maybe he could also send the plans to the Mayor, with a letter explaining the project properly. After all, if the Mayor understood the *chambre d'hôte* would bring business into the village, he might help the plans through the bureaucratic tangle.

The sweat prickled on Brian's forehead. The sun began to touch the dormer window, warming the room. He wiped his glasses with his handkerchief, finished his glass of wine and retrieved the bottle that he'd hidden among the books. Thus fortified, he started a letter to the Mayor. His mind kept returning to Alison's job-hunting. Perhaps he ought to look for a job himself. The idea filled him with horror. He wasn't really a lazy man. After all he'd replaced the shutters on the house himself and done a lot of decorating. It was simply the idea of employment that horrified him.

He hadn't forgotten the argument he'd had with his boss not long before he'd left the Greenaway Agency. By then, he was working in an office block built of glass and steel, which gave the impression of having no walls, only windows from which he could see the traffic in the street beneath. The odd little rooms he remembered from his earlier jobs had gone, to be replaced by groups of desks in an open plan area. Only senior people got individual offices.

He'd been working for an advert for a deodorant, the message of which had made him groan. Show a man who's active, sporty and yet wants to be clean and attractive enough to sweep the girls off their feet. How to be sporty and romantic at the same time, without being clichéd? He messed about with phrases and pieces of dialogue, before settling for four lines of verse.

"You can run the pitch and seek to score
Then be clean and fresh the Wavefresh way
To meet the girl in white once more
And dine with her at the end of the day."

His boss, Jay Masterson, called him into his office. He was sitting back in his chair, with his paunch overflowing his desk and Brian's copy open on his computer. Having checked his tie, Brian sat opposite, trying to stay poised enough to look alert without being rigid.

"This copy for the Wavefresh ad is crap," Jay said. "Can't you come up with anything better?"

"I was doing what you asked for. Combining the thrill of sport with romance."

"But it's verse. It's so out of date. Today's audience wants something crisper."

Brian blinked. "Can romance be crisp?"

"Of course it can. It's just the question of finding the right words. That's what you're supposed to be good at. Words." Jay pushed his chair back, then leaned forward until his elbows rested on the desk. The position expressed menace. "If you ask me, Brian, you're past it. You're not coming up with good ideas any longer. If you don't pull your socks up, you'll be out. Now go and redo that ad."

Brian lurched out of the office and walked back to his desk, conscious of the polished young men and women working at their computers. One of the girls smiled and he thought she was laughing at him. He loathed them for their arrogant belief in their own cleverness, their assurance that life would load them with rewards, while he struggled. From that day on, he had fretted to be free. Having escaped, he wasn't going to return to that servitude. If he was going to work, it would have to be a form of self employment.

It occurred to him that if he and Alison struggled with French, surely people here might have similar problems with English. The grammar might be less rigid but English spelling was a nightmare. Surely, there must be French families in the area who'd be prepared to pay for a few hours per week of English tuition. The more he considered the idea, the more attractive it appeared. He remembered how much they'd paid Dubois to help Steve with his French. With enough French to make himself understood and perfect English, it shouldn't be too difficult to earn some money as a tutor.

Brian sat back in his chair and imagined the scene. He would sit at a desk with a young French boy and a pile of books and papers, imparting his knowledge and love of the English language. Of course, he'd have to plan lessons but that shouldn't be too difficult. Shakespeare and Dickens would be too difficult to start with, so he would find easy materials and work up. It would be an excellent job for him. He'd write an advert offering his services, display it at a local newsagent and see what happened.

*

Brian was framing his advert when he heard Alison's feet on the stairs. With a surreptitious gesture, he slipped the pile of bills and letters from creditors under a file.

"I've got a job," Alison said. She stood opposite the desk, like a schoolgirl seeking approval from a teacher.

"What?"

"At a restaurant – Le Pont, down by the river. We've eaten there. I don't know if you remember it. I'll be washing up."

"Washing up?" Brian's sense of shock resonated in his voice. Alison was slim and almost delicate-looking with her pale skin and long fingers. He couldn't help thinking his wife was too good for a menial job like that. Although she did it at home.

"I'm starting on Saturday. From ten to three, then a break, then five 'til late."

"Late?" He ran his hand through his hair, as he wondered how he and Steve would manage in her absence.

"You'll have to get dinner for yourself and Steve. But I can get some ready made things in. I'm not working every evening, anyway. Le Pont isn't open Sundays or Mondays."

"Will you need the car?" An appalling thought occurred to him. Without the car, he'd be marooned in the village, unable to go shopping in Caillac or visit Carrie in Beaumont. And he wouldn't be able to work as a tutor for more than a couple of hours a week.

"Of course."

"I was going to advertise my services as an English tutor. I'm sure I could earn more than you could washing up."

"You didn't tell me that," said Alison, drawing up the spare chair that stood near the door.

"I think tutoring would suit me very well. I love the English language. I should be able to impart some of that enthusiasm to a willing French child."

She laughed. "You a tutor? Have you looked at yourself lately? You'd need to sober up and you'd need to be reliable."

His mouth gaped open. Her amusement shook his dawning confidence. It had never occurred to him that Alison, who'd always been so supportive, might mock his idea. He stood up, as his surprise turned to anger, then into a new determination to prove himself capable of carrying out his plan. "I'll show you. I'll advertise. I'll get a job as a tutor and you can forget washing up."

She shrugged. "We'll see."

Chapter 9

Le Pont was filled with the sounds and smells of cooking when Alison arrived in the middle of Saturday morning. François, transformed by his chef's whites, stood stripping fat from a piece of beef. A plump man stood at a hob, sweat gleaming on his face, as he stirred a mound of chopped onion. A tall youth with straw-like hair worked at the preparation table, cutting open red peppers. Alison stood in the doorway, reluctant to intrude.

François smiled and put down his knife. "I'm glad you're early. We'll be busy soon."

Although he had given Alison a tour of the restaurant, he hadn't shown her where cleaning things were kept. She found aprons stacked neatly on a shelf near the door, but had to rummage in a cupboard near the sink for rubber gloves and washing up liquid. By the time she was ready, the plump chef had placed a steaming frying pan on the work surface.

Alison filled the sink with hot water, producing a cloud of vapour. The view through the window, of the boats moored on the Lot, blurred and disappeared. As the chefs worked, a thread of conversation wove between the rattle of pans and the sizzle of frying. Sudden bursts of flame rose from pans and the scents of oil and garlic mingled with those of searing meat, herbs and spices. Extractor fans whirred and an electric fly killer near the ceiling crackled. The heat from ovens and hobs sent the temperature soaring.

Pans and utensils arrived faster on the work surface. Although cutlery and bowls went into the dishwasher, the pans were thick with fat and cooking juices. As Alison scrubbed, grease trickled down her arms and sweat down her back. Before long, her wrists and legs ached. Although she tried shifting her position, it made little difference.

François shouted : *"La sauce, vite. Maintenant!"*

It seemed an age before the pile of pans and utensils waiting to be washed dwindled. Through the steam, she became aware of Nathalie standing nearby. She looked pretty and confident in black skirt, white blouse and silver hoop earrings, ready to start work as a waitress. Alison realised how dirty she must look after only part of the day's work.

Nathalie winked at her. "The last assistant survived three weeks. I hope you do better."

"Thanks." Alison wondered if her comment was intended to be friendly.

"Lunch is ready. Upstairs."

Alison nodded and took her rubber gloves off with relief. Behind one of the doors marked *privé* she'd found a staff cloakroom where she washed her face and ran a comb through her hair. Feeling a little cleaner, she trudged up the stone stairs to the restaurant. François was sitting at the table nearest to the stairs with other members of staff. Two big bowls of penne in a cream sauce full of mushrooms and ham stood in the centre of the table, along with bottles of red wine and carafes of water.

Nathalie stood next to the tall blond youth. "Has Papa introduced you?" she asked.

Alison shook her head.

"Maman would have remembered." Nathalie touched the shoulder of the young man. "This is Pierre. He's just starting out."

Pierre nodded.

She waved a hand in the direction of the plump man: "This is Gérard, he's the sous chef."

As Gérard smiled, his eyes disappeared.

François nodded at Alison: the first time since preparation started in earnest he'd paid any attention to her. "Sit down. You've deserved a rest."

She took an empty chair, sat down and looked at her neighbours. The group resembled a family gathering, at which she knew few people. It was easy to feel like an intruder. She helped herself to pasta and listened to the conversation. There were snatches she could understand : *"Je vais aller au match..." "le vin est trop cher..."* However she lost the thread when the pace picked up, or several people spoke at once.

From where she sat, she could see the balcony that occupied the whole of one wall, but not the river Lot which lay beyond. That didn't stop her wishing she was on one of the white boats, paddling her feet in the river. The water would be so cool. Dismissing the fantasy, she turned her attention to the interior of the restaurant. Next to the entrance to the bar stood a heavy oak dresser, laden with glasses and cups. The rest of the décor looked more modern and someone had paid attention to the colour scheme. The walls were painted cream, while the dark red tablecloths matched the upholstery of the chairs. In alcoves there were old black and white photographs of local scenes. One showed the bridge that gave the restaurant its name – Le Pont – and cars from the 1920s or 30s. If François had chosen the colour scheme and the pictures, he was a man of some taste.

She wondered about the comment Nathalie had made about her mother while introducing the chefs. It seemed that Madame Allombert was absent. There could be any number of reasons for that: she might be visiting relatives, or ill, or she could have died or left permanently. If François was struggling to run the restaurant without the support of his wife, Alison's sympathy went out to him.

Once the meal was over, staff members trooped back down the stairs and took up their places to start service. Pierre heated prepared food in an industrial microwave, and placed the hot dishes in the food lift. The riot of noise and bustle returned to the kitchen. After a while, the succession of pots and utensils arriving on the work surfaces blurred. In the midst of the confusion, she tipped up a pan she was holding and fat dribbled onto the floor. François thrust a mop at her.

"Clean it up."

Taken aback by the abruptness of his tone, Alison's self-possession wavered. She took the mop but stood holding it, while the smells and noise around her whirled into chaos.

François watched her for a moment, then laid his hand gently on her shoulder. *"Ça va?"* he asked.

She nodded, relieved by his kindly response. Although he might snap at his staff during the rush of work, he wasn't unfeeling.

Eventually, she noticed other staff wandering out of the kitchen and talking in the hallway. She finished washing up, took the mop, and started cleaning the quarry-tiled floor. But, after she'd completed a few sweeps, François took the mop from her.

"You have survived. Will you come back this evening?"

"Of course."

"Good."

Alison stepped out of the kitchen door. The river glittered in the afternoon sun and the quiet was soothing after the bustle and noise of the restaurant. Gérard was sitting in the shade on the patio, with a beer in one hand and a cigarette in the other. For a moment she was tempted to stay here and relax, but she reminded herself that she'd promised to return home. Steve had told her Brian had burned the dinner while she was away and she wanted to check there hadn't been another mishap.

***

On Sunday, Brian had an interview with Christophe Favard. He drove down the hill, across a little stream at the bottom of the valley and up the ridge on the far side. Although he found the house without difficulty, he drove past and stopped on a track beside a field of maize. He drew a packet of Marlboros from the glove box, lit one and composed himself.

It had proved easy to post an advert in the newsagent offering his services as a tutor. He'd done so in a rush of anger – he had to prove Alison wrong, as her dismissal of his idea that he could be a good tutor filled him with resentment. When Favard rang to say he wanted someone to teach English to his twelve year old son Léon, Brian's morale rose. For the first time since the disastrous arrival of the Mayor, something positive had happened. But Alison's derision left its mark - prompting him to take care with his appearance, combing his thinning hair and choosing a cream shirt to wear with brown chinos. And he'd drunk no alcohol that morning. He sat in the car for a minute telling himself Alison was wrong and he'd be a great tutor.

Favard's villa stood on top of the ridge almost opposite St. Thomas. Brian could see across the valley, with a line of trees along the stream, to the village with its white church in the distance. The house itself was recent, covered in a cream rendering. The traditional shutters had been scrapped but a porch added, supported on mock Ionic columns. Brian thought them pretentious.

When he rang the doorbell, it was answered by a young girl with fair curls and a pink dress.

He smiled at her. "Hallo. Is your Papa in?"

She ran back into the house and returned with a middle aged man with glasses and a neat moustache. He greeted Brian with a frown before substituting a half-hearted smile. "Thank you for coming on a Sunday." Favard shook hands. "It's about the only day I can be at home."

"I'm sure we're both busy men," said Brian, aware it wasn't true of him. In fact, he'd been glad when Favard suggested Sunday, one of the few days he had the car. He reckoned that, if Favard offered him employment, he could negotiate a time on Monday, when Alison would be at home. Or convince her it made more sense for him to be working as a tutor than for her to wash up in Le Pont. Though, if there was enough money in it, he'd buy a second car.

As Brian stepped into the hall, he nearly fell over a child's scooter lying on the carpet. The top of a low cupboard by the nearest wall was piled high with balls of various sizes, plastic racquets and cycle helmets.

"I want Léon to learn good English," said Favard, leading the way into the living room, furnished with elegant blue-grey armchairs. "But I don't have much time with the children. I run a business, selling office furniture."

Brian stood, feeling awkward, until Favard gestured to one of the armchairs. "Of course English is an important language. A language of business as well as literature." He looked out of a patio door, through a verandah draped with trailing vines, to a garden beyond. The fair haired girl he'd seen earlier was sitting on a swing under an apple tree. The scene looked idyllic.

"What qualifications do you have, Monsieur Delaney?" asked Favard.

Brian nodded. " I'm a native English speaker and I've got a degree in English from the University of Kent."

"Good, good. But do you also have a teaching qualification?"

Brian was considering how to reply when a scream came from the garden. Both men stood up. The little girl was lying on the grass under the swing, while a blond boy stood nearby, his bicycle propped against the apple tree.

"Léon, did you push her?" shouted Favard. He opened the patio door, strode into the garden and grabbed the boy's arm.

Brian stood near the window, uncertain how to react. He wondered if his duties would include looking after the little girl as well as teaching her brother. Although he'd helped Steve with his homework, he'd never had to deal with more than one child at a time. He wasn't sure he liked the prospect.

As Favard comforted his daughter and remonstrated with his son, Brian looked round the room. A large flat screen television occupied the centre of one wall, while the cabinet opposite exhibited a collection of jade ornaments, and the cream carpet had a luxurious deep pile. These people had money. Brian begin to increase the price he felt he could charge for his services.

After a few minutes, Favard returned, dragging Léon by the arm. The boy's blond hair fell over his eyes and his mouth was twisted into an expression of reluctance. The men sat down again, leaving the boy standing and fidgeting, scraping at a brown mark on his elbow which looked like dried blood.

"Say something to Monsieur Delaney in English," Favard told his son.

"Good morning Monsieur Delaney," Léon said in a sing-song fashion.

Brian smiled. "Good morning. Do you like English ?"

The boy stared at Brian for a few moments, looked at his father and shrugged.

"All right. Go and play now, but leave Sylvie alone."

Favard watched Léon hurry out of the room, then turned back to Brian. "You were telling me about your teaching qualifications."

Brian assumed as much confidence as he could muster. "I taught at my son's school in London."

"What age group?"

"Sixth form." Brian could imagine himself teaching a class of interested sixth formers. They would pay attention, ask intelligent questions, appreciate his opinions.

Favard frowned. "That's not much use. I'm looking for someone who's taught eleven and twelve year olds. "

"I'm sure I could teach Léon, Monsieur Favard,"said Brian, with an effort at humility. "I worked in advertising most of my career and I'm good at choosing the right language for the audience."

Favard rose. "That won't do. I'm looking for somebody who has teaching qualifications and experience. I'm not going to leave my son's education to just anybody."

"I've had a number of responsible jobs," said Brian, but it was no use. Favard was standing by the door to the hall, ready to show him out.

Brian hurried back to the car and drove off, grasping the steering wheel hard. He'd been made to look a complete charlatan. Of course, he shouldn't have tried to lie but all he wanted was a chance to prove himself. Everyone was against him. First the Mayor said no to his reasonable proposals for redeveloping the barns, then Favard turned him down as a tutor for his son. He was angry with Favard, who gave every indication of being full of self-importance. A more modest man might have been less demanding. On top of his disappointment, Brian faced the prospect of admitting his failure to Alison. It filled him with so much anguish, he decided against going straight home. Instead, he turned towards Caillac with the view of drowning his sorrows in a bar.

***

Alison had hoped to relax on Sunday evening and use the time to ring her mother. When Brian arrived home the worse for drink, she had to listen to him raging about the stupidity of other people. She told him off for driving under the influence and he stumped up to the writer's room. Would her rebuke make a difference? She doubted it. Since the Mayor said '*non*', Brian's drinking had increased, and she wasn't sure how far she could trust him to do tasks like shopping without stopping at a café. That, as well as his failure to get this job, confirmed her view that she needed to take charge in the household.

Worrying about Brian's bad temper didn't help, as she wondered what to say to her mother. How would she explain her decision to work in a restaurant? Alison sat at the desk in the living room, doodling on the notepad next to the phone. In the subdued evening light, the sand colour of the armchairs faded to beige, and the copper chimney cover to plain brown.

At least the house was in a better state than in their early days. The place had been dirty and dilapidated: not only cobwebs everywhere and mould in the main bedroom but a rat's nest under the front door. It had been so cold in the winter they had lived in the kitchen. The barn had been full of junk, including an old Citroen CV and a pickled snake in a jar. However, the arguments they'd had concerned minor things. Brian had wanted propane gas for cooking, because it was cheaper than electricity.

"Isn't it dangerous?" she'd asked.

"Not unless it leaks or someone sets fire to it."

"Well you'd better not smoke then."

Brian had usually won the arguments and they had made great improvements. But spent too much money. There was a thud of heavy metal music from Steve's room, which reminded Alison of her task.

The phone was answered promptly. Alison had an image of her mother sitting in one of her armchairs, with a cat on her lap.

"How are you, Mum?"

"I had a problem with the overflow. It was running and I had to get a plumber. He had to go up in the loft and you know what it's like up there. Boxes and things everywhere."

Alison suppressed a sigh, realising she couldn't do anything to help Daphne. "Did you manage to get it sorted?"

"In the end. But I feel so useless in the house on my own. There's so many things I can't do."

"Is there anyone who can give you a hand?" Alison asked, though she guessed the answer.

"Not really. Not with you in France and Tim in Bristol."

Alison was never sure whether her mother was trying to make her feel guilty, or whether her complaints were simply a product of dissatisfaction. Nevertheless, she tried to resist guilt, telling herself she was doing well to cope with her daily life. The strategy didn't work. As she thought of a reply, Steve opened his door to wander through the living room, leaving a blast of sound.

Alison clamped her hand over the phone's mouthpiece. "Steve, can you shut your door!" Once the door was closed, she returned to the phone.

Her mother was half-way though a sentence. "...isn't going to get any easier. I've half a mind to sell this house and move somewhere smaller. It's too big for me."

"Would you move nearer to Tim's?" Alison considered the suggestion. It would make sense, but she wondered how her mother would cope with dealing with estate agents and solicitors. James had taken all the major decisions and there might be people who would trick Daphne.

"I don't want to leave Bromley. But it would be easier to manage a flat."

"That sounds a good idea. But don't let anyone talk you into doing something you'd regret."

"I'm not going to jump into things. I've been on my own here since your father died,"said Daphne, annoyance in her voice.

"I'm sure Tim could advise," Alison said, conciliatory. For a moment, she hesitated, aware of the need to tell her mother about her own circumstances. She worried that Daphne would find the opportunity for another piece of veiled criticism. "Mum, I was going to say I'm working in a restaurant some days. If you ring in the evening you might not get me."

Alison watched Steve ambling back across the living room, munching a piece of bread he'd taken from the kitchen. She nodded to thank him for closing the door.

"Working in a restaurant?" said Daphne. " That's good. You're quite a cook."

Alison decided not to disillusion her mother about the nature of her work. She let the matter rest, rang off and went to sit in one of the armchairs. The house in Bromley had been such an important part of her childhood, it seemed strange to think of it being sold. Even here, in France, she could remember every room, and invest each place with memories. She realised that, for her mother, leaving the house she'd shared with her husband would be a devastating break with the past. If she was thinking of making the move, she must be desperate. As so often, after conversations with her mother, Alison was overcome by a sense of grief. She had let Daphne down.

Chapter 10

After a week working at Le Pont, Alison recognised the rhythms of the restaurant's day. The flurry of noise and activity slowed as the end of lunchtime service approached. Gérard and Pierre drifted into the hallway and stood chatting. Only François remained, moving in and out of the refrigerator, checking stocks. Alison cleaned the last trace of fat off a pan and left it to drain, then mopped the floor and stowed the mop in its bucket. Although she was aching for a break, she wanted his permission to leave her post. He was always busy, she knew that, and she was the lowliest member of staff, but she liked him to notice her.

In the end, she asked "Can I go now?"

He put a jar of sauce down on the counter used for plating-up and nodded. *"Bien sûr.* Are you going to sit outside?"

"I might go for a walk by the river first." After the first afternoon, she'd decided it wasn't worth returning home to find Steve missing and Brian drunk, argumentative or both. It was easier and pleasanter to stay in Caillac.

François smiled. "I might see you outside."

When Alison opened the back door, there was no-one sitting on the patio. She looked towards the bridge and the town centre, then walked the other way. To her left, the Lot idled so slowly the only discernible movement was a creasing round the arches of the bridge. A few people lazed on the motor cruisers moored along the bank. To her right, patio gardens, or pots of bright geraniums, stood behind each shop. A woman who was watering the planters behind the neighbouring flower shop stood up and said *'Bonjour Madame'*. The sound of traffic on the bridge dwindled. After a few minutes, Alison came to a bend in the river, where the roadway stopped at a slipway which led down into the water.

As Alison ambled back to the restaurant, she saw François and Nathalie sitting at a metal table on the patio. Nathalie was twisting a lock of hair round her finger and François's eyebrows were bunched together. It looked like a family dispute. There was a clear resemblance between father and daughter, although Nathalie's nose was gently curved, while her father's was beaked. Reluctant to intrude into a private conversation, Alison turned to walk towards the bridge.

François looked up. "Come and join us. I've asked for *jus d'orange* from the bar."

She found a chair near a planter full of orange marigolds, which marked the edge of the patio.

"Have you any children, Alison?" asked François.

"One son, who's called Stephen."

François nodded. "My son Philippe is in Paris, learning to be a gourmet chef."

Alison noticed the pride in his voice and realised this man, who seemed so focused on his work, was also a caring father.

Nathalie scowled. "I don't want to work in the restaurant business."

"Then you need to decide what you want to do," said François, sternly.

A waiter appeared from the kitchen door, with a tray holding glasses and a carafe of orange juice, and put it on the table.

Alison poured herself a glass, and wondered what Steve would do when he finished school.

François sat with his glass in his hand, considering. "Nathalie wants to go to Castelnau with friends on Saturday evening. Do you think I should let her, Alison?"

Alison wondered why François was turning to her for advice, when there were doubtless female relatives, or waitresses he could consult. Maybe she was simply in the right place at the right time; maybe he felt the waitresses were too young to be reliable. But she was glad he was trying to get to know her.

"What are you going to do in Castelnau?" she asked Nathalie, feeling some sympathy with her. Before Steve met André, he'd complained there was nothing to do in Caillac. Castelnau had more entertainment.

"We're going to the disco," said Nathalie.

"Is someone taking you?"

"My friend Lucie's mother."

"I don't want you hanging around in Castelnau in the evening," said François. "You never know who you might meet."

Nathalie ran her finger round the rim of her glass, producing a whining noise.

"Do you mean the disco that's part of the *Fête de la Bastide?*" Alison asked. In this case many young people would be going. Although she understood François's concern for his daughter's safety, she guessed he could afford to relax a little. Had Madame Allombert been at home, she might have been more comfortable dealing with her daughter. If François was on his own, he might struggle to understand the interests of a teenage girl. "I think Steve's going with his friend André." Alison noticed a slight smile on Nathalie's lips and wondered about its cause.

"It's more difficult for a girl," said François, shaking his head. "If Philippe was here, it would be OK."

"I think Nathalie will be all right if she doesn't stay too late. Is Lucie's mother going to pick you up afterwards Nathalie?"

"Yeah."

"What time?"

"Eleven."

François looked from Alison to his daughter and nodded. *"Eh bien."*

Nathalie's smile transformed her face from sullen to beautiful. "Thanks."

Alison hoped she had acquired a friend. Nathalie might be only young but she was *le patron's* daughter, which might give her influence. In this unfamiliar place, the more allies she could make, the better. She wondered if father and daughter were struggling to adjust to life without Madame Allombert and if she could offer any support. Not that her own family was any kind of model.

The kitchen door opened, Pierre appeared and Nathalie rose. "I'm going into town with Pierre."

"You'll be back in time for afternoon prep?" asked François, raising his eyebrows.

"Of course."

Nathalie joined Pierre and they started walking along the drive towards the bridge. Pierre was so tall, he leaned towards her to diminish the height difference. Alison wondered what the relationship was between them. To her Pierre seemed gauche and she guessed he was little more than eighteen.

François sighed. "I worry about her."

She nodded. "I understand. I worry about Steve." Concern about Steve was the constant note that threaded through the hubbub of her other worries. She looked down at the marigolds and considered whether to ask the question on her mind. "Can I ask if you're on your own?"

"Simone left nearly a year ago. She had another man." He sank his head into his hands. The tip of the middle finger of his left hand was missing."It made me angry for a long time."

"I'm sorry."

He looked up. " Nathalie thinks it was my fault. She says I make everyone work too hard. Maybe she's right."

"Of course you have to work." Alison thought of Brian, who wasn't working at all. Perhaps she understood François's attitude better.

Gérard emerged from the kitchen door, a glass in his hand. "Some of us were thinking of playing bridge in the bar. Do you want to join us?"

François nodded. "Tell them I'll be there in a minute." After Gérard disappeared, he lay his hand over Alison's. "I'm sorry to trouble you with my problems, Alison. I'm sure you have enough of your own."

"I'm glad you feel you can talk to me. And don't worry about Nathalie. I'm sure she'll be all right." Alison removed her hand. She didn't think François was a groper, unlike Gérard, whom she'd seen patting Nathalie's bottom as she passed. François's gesture seemed more one of appreciation. It pleased her.

***

In the centre of Castelnau, the daytime events of the *Fête de la Bastide* were giving way to evening ones. Red and blue pennants were strung across the square and, now the sun was setting, they had been joined by floodlights, which played on the church in the centre, making the old bricks glow red and bronze. Tables and benches spread out from a restaurant underneath the arcade, filling the whole square with people enjoying their meals. A band played on the church steps and children ran between tables. Steve joined the crowd of young people outside a large hall at one corner of the square.

He followed, as André edged into the hall. Although people gave way to André because of his size, he stopped from time to time to talk to friends. Steve tried to join in the conversations but sometimes failed because André knew more people than he did. Stars of various colours and sizes hung from the ceiling. The hall had a dais at one end, loaded with speakers, cables and lights. A man with spiked hair and a black shirt open to the waist was fiddling with a microphone. Maybe he was trying to look cool but Steve wasn't impressed. This place was provincial compared to South London.

Leaving André chatting, Steve made his way to a table at the other end of the hall, where two middle-aged men were presiding over a bar. They looked out of place with moustaches and check shirts. Steve tried to buy a beer but one of the men stared at him and shook his head. For a few moments, Steve stood disappointed, before settling for an orange juice. At least he had some money, which Georges Ricaud had slipped him at the end of the peach harvest. It was humiliating to be so often broke.

Gradually, the hall filled with guys and girls in tight jeans. Although he'd washed his hair and worn his red T-shirt bearing the words *Route 66*, Steve was aware his jeans were too long. His mother would never accept that French teenagers wore theirs short. After a while, the DJ welcomed everyone to the disco and announced the beginning of the music. Floodlights filled the room with blue and white light and music blared from speakers. A few girls broke away from the crowd and started dancing, swaying and gyrating. Among them Steve recognised Nathalie. She looked beautiful and sexy in a silver top with black jeans and pendant earrings. Steve put his glass down on a table and wondered if he dared step into the space round the dancers and join her. The guys were standing round the edges of the gathering, watching the girls. Steve sized them up. Many looked bigger or cooler than him and he didn't rate his chances.

As more people began to dance, André walked between them and started dancing next to Nathalie. André wasn't a natural dancer, being awkward compared to Nathalie, but she smiled at him. Although Steve had grown used to his friend's popularity, he resented André's success. Why shouldn't he win Nathalie himself? To mask a growing anger, Steve turned back towards the bar table, as if to buy another orange juice.

He met Amélie moving towards the dancers. She wasn't as pretty as Nathalie, with her round face and plump buttocks but she was smiling at him. Not wanting to look left out, he followed her into the centre of the floor, which was growing crowded. He swayed and turned opposite Amélie until one track faded into another, the crowd eddied and he found himself facing Nathalie.

Her eyes shone with laughter. "Hallo, peach thrower!"

Steve grinned back. At least she remembered him, if only because of the incident in the orchard. He struggled for something clever to say and failed.

She smiled, tossed her dark hair and started dancing opposite him.

Steve felt he ought to say something to her but didn't know what. "I like your top," he said after a while.

She pointed at his T-shirt. "Why Route 66? D'you want to go there?"

Steve hesitated, aware that his chances of travelling were nil at present. "It's only a road. But I know London."

"That's not America."

"It's a great city. I could take you there."

She laughed.

He gave up trying to talk because the music was thundering out of the speakers at a volume that made it almost impossible to hear. It was enough to be close to Nathalie, breathing in the scent she wore and feeling the warmth of her breath on his face. He paid no attention when the next track began and was pleased when Nathalie continued dancing with him. Maybe he'd been wrong when he thought Nathalie preferred André. At last he was enjoying himself.

After a while, the pace of the music slowed and the crowd reorganised itself.

Nathalie turned away from him. "See you sometime."

"At *lycée*?"

"OK."

Steve watched Nathalie disappear into the crowd, then found his way back to the bar, flushed with pleasure and success.

Chapter 11

Brian was feeling mellow. He'd spent a couple of hours in the orchard, picking the purple plums that drooped from the old trees. When they first came to France, the plum harvest had been a family event, when he'd teetered on a ladder, tossing down plums, while Alison held a bowl and Steve foraged underneath the tree, picking up fallen fruit. Alison had made pies and jam, prizing the small mirabelle plums, which proved the sweetest. Since then, he'd pruned the trees, cutting back dead branches and using them for firewood. This year, plums were plentiful, but Alison wouldn't have time to make jam. Brian saw an opportunity to prove himself as capable as his wife.

Fetching a step ladder, he planted it in rough grass at the base of a tree and climbed. As he worked, the sun rose higher, until the garden simmered in light and heat. He left a bottle of Armagnac at the base of the tree, and sat on the grass for a while each time he descended, enjoying a swig of brandy and a cigarette in the shade. Thus restored, he did another spell of work. After a long lunch break, he decided he'd done enough and left two large bowls of plums on a work surface in the kitchen. Although he intended to jam them later, he climbed the stairs to the writer's room and relaxed.

He was woken from a doze by Steve opening the door, As usual, after a day at André's, Steve looked brown and tired.

"Have a good day?" Brian asked.

"Fine. We went swimming in the reservoir."

Brian gazed at his son, envying his energy.

Steve drew up the old, wooden chair which was the only other place to sit in the writing room. "André's papa has bought him a scooter. Any chance of you getting me one?"

"How much are they?"

"Three hundred Euros."

Brian took his glasses off and polished them, as he thought about bills he couldn't pay. "Look, Steve, we haven't got the money."

"I'll have to cycle to the *lycée*," Steve said in an aggrieved tone. "Even in the rain."

"You can get the bus."

"None of my mates use the bus."

"I used to get the bus to school," Brian said, remembering the crowd of school and college students that had lurked around the bus stop at the end of his road. He didn't add that he'd been beaten up by boys from the comprehensive.

"That was ages ago. Are we never going to have any money?"

Brian sighed. "We'd have been all right if the bloody Mayor hadn't turned us down..."

Steve pushed back his chair, rose and pressed his knuckles on the desk. In this position, he was large and intimidating. "No. You got us into this mess. You could have gone on working in London. Or you could have looked for a proper job here. As it is, Mum's working all hours and you're sitting on your arse."

Brian's face reddened and he stood up to face his son. "Don't you dare talk to me like that."

"It's true."

"No it's not, I've been working. I've been picking plums."

Steve snorted. "What are you going to do with them? I don't think I'd trust you to cook them, not after that time you burned the dinner." At the door, he turned and glowered. "I'd like to see you cycling everywhere like I do." He slammed the door behind him.

Brian's hand trembled so much, as he poured himself another glass of wine, he spilled a little. He had the uncomfortable feeling he was losing control of his household. Neither his wife nor his son treated him with the respect he deserved. They were forgetting the work he'd done, both in London and in the house here, and they were ignoring the fact that his freedom was limited while Alison used the car. But Steve's parting words made him think. If Steve could cycle to Caillac, why couldn't he do so himself? There was an old bicycle in the barn and, if he got it working, it might provide him with a means of transport.

*

When Brian got up the next morning, he found a scribbled message from Alison: " I hope you're going to jam these plums. I won't have time." Although this did nothing to improve Brian's morale, it didn't deter him from the task of restoring his bicycle. He'd deal with the plums later. With this thought in mind, he opened the big wooden doors at the end of the barn. This area had been earmarked for storage, with a wall between it and the bedrooms of the *chambre d'hôte*. He looked with regret at the concrete floor, which had cost so much to lay. The two bikes stacked in a corner were covered in cobwebs. A selection of tools lay in a toolbox nearby, many of them rusty. Steve's bike was missing and Brian remembered his son had said he was going to look for kingfishers.

Brian took his old blue bike out onto the gravel drive and examined it. The brakes needed adjusting and the chain oiling, but the bike seemed sound. The tyres were flat but, once he'd pumped them up, he decided they'd be good enough for a trial run. He crouched on the gravel, surrounded by bottles of oil, Allen keys, and an old pump. There were times when he was grateful to his father for teaching him practical skills. Although he'd despised Eddie for his limited interests in life: lorries, beer and women, he had to admit his father could make or mend almost anything. Some of those skills had proved useful when they'd bought the house. He could certainly get a bike working.

Once he'd finished, Brian decided to cycle down the hill and along the main road for a while. Before setting out, he filled a rucksack with a spare tyre, other tools and a bottle of Armagnac in case he felt in need of refreshment. He pushed his bike to the gate, and free-wheeled down the hill. It was a pleasure to bowl along with the wind on his face, passing plum orchards and fields where sunflower heads hung dark and heavy, ready for harvest. He remembered cycling in the Addington Hills as a boy and some of the uncomplicated joy of childhood returned.

The road levelled at the junction at the bottom of the hill and Brian turned right to cycle in the direction of Caillac. When he reached a grove of poplars, he decided he'd gone far enough and turned round. Once he got back to the road to St Thomas he began to pedal up the hill. As he climbed, he tired, his progress slowed and the bike wove from side to side. Refusing to admit defeat, he rose on the pedals and strained his leg muscles. At last, he wobbled to a halt, struggling for breath. Overcome by frustration, he threw the bike on the bank, where it lay among sunflowers, pedals spinning. He sat on the bank gasping, reached for the bottle of Armagnac and took a swig.

As Brian sat drinking, he saw a cyclist, dressed in jeans, a T shirt and a red helmet, riding up the hill. Steve. Brian felt a sudden lurch of envy, as Steve was climbing strongly. He drew level, stopped and dismounted.

"You all right, Dad?" he asked.

"Just taking my time and enjoying the view," Brian said, assuming an air of nonchalance.

Steve looked at the bottle of Armagnac and snorted. "You mean you couldn't get up the hill and now you're drunk."

Brian lurched to his feet. "I'm not drunk. I rode quite a long way and thought I'd have a rest on the way home."

"You can hardly stand up."

"Who are you to critcise? You're just a boy." Angered by Steve's contemptuous tone, Brian struggled to regain his authority.

Steve peered to left and right, as if expecting to see someone. "I wouldn't want my friends to see you with me."

"Damn your cheek!" The anger and frustration in Brian's mind knotted into an overpowering temptation to hit his son's sunburnt nose. He aimed a blow but was slow and awkward, allowing time for Steve to reach out a brown arm and push. Brian fell on his back on the bank, losing his glasses and landing in a flurry of earth and sunflower leaves.

Steve pulled him up by an arm, picked up his glasses and brushed leaves off his shirt. " Sorry, Dad. I didn't mean to hurt you. I just want you to stop drinking." He climbed on his bike, then hesitated. " You better walk up this hill. It's steep."

Brian stood, watching Steve riding up the hill until he disappeared round the corner. He felt shaken and disconsolate, weighed down by a sense that nothing in his life was working out. Worse, he was aware his relationship with his son had changed irrevocably. The argument reminded him of the films he'd seen where the old male lion was defeated by a newcomer and retired hurt. Was that happening to him?

Chapter 12

Crowds eddied and surged round the gate of the *lycée genérale,* an array of white rectangular blocks in parkland on the outskirts of Caillac. Steve threaded his way between his fellow pupils, watching the youths on scooters with a frisson of envy. It would have been wonderful to ride a shiny new scooter, but his father had made it clear he couldn't afford one. In theory, he could have caught the school bus but that would have been humiliating. The bus was for younger ones. So he'd pulled on his helmet, stuffed a waterproof jacket in his rucksack in case it rained, and assured his mother he would cope.

Having started the second year, he was happy to be at *lycée.* An uneasy atmosphere lingered at home. Mum was often tired after working at Le Pont and Dad either drunk or irritable, or both. Not only would going to school keep him out of arguments, but also give him a chance of seeing Nathalie. He'd found out from Amélie what classes Nathalie was in and intended to look for her. To be happy about going to school was progress.

As he pushed his bicycle towards the rack, he remembered his traumatic first year at a French school. On his first day at the *collége* his mother had dropped him off at the gate. He'd walked into the playground, carrying a bag of sports equipment and one of books, and stopped. This was hostile territory. A crowd of French boys overtook him. They jostled, laughed and bombarded him with questions.

"Where did you get those weird shoes?"

"What football team do you support?"

He watched them, only half understanding, and couldn't reply. The curiosity was replaced by mockery.

"*Crétin.*"

They taunted and prodded him all the way to the school building. Only the presence of a teacher stopped the onslaught.

In lessons, he fared little better, sitting at his desk and letting the teacher's words float over him. He tried bunking off, but found it boring roaming the streets of Caillac on his own. It was easier to sit at his desk and doodle in his notebooks. Art was the only lesson he liked. He railed at his parents, accusing them of setting him up to fail, and they responded by paying for M. Dubois to provide him with additional French lessons. Steve resented the drilling he received from Dubois and described him as an old tyrant. But his lessons made the difference. At the end of the *Troisième*, Steve managed to get the grades required to move on to the *lycée*.

Fortunately, the *lycée* proved better. He made friends with André Ricaud, and did well enough to prove that he wasn't as stupid as some of his classmates had said. In theory he could leave, now he was sixteen. Shortly after his birthday in February he'd told his mother he was thinking of doing so. For once, she had been sitting in the living room, sewing buttons onto his father's shirt. He sat and fiddled with a cotton reel until she looked up.

"Look, Mum, I know we're short of money. I could leave school, get a job in a supermarket or something."

She let the shirt drop onto the chair arm. "No Steve, please don't. I wish I hadn't left school at sixteen."

"Don't know if there's any point staying." Steve didn't believe his father, who'd gone to university, had done better at work than his mother. But he didn't say so.

"You should get your *bac*. That'll give you more opportunities."

He snorted. "What, here?"

"Not just here. Even if you go back to England a *bac* would count."

Steve hadn't been convinced but, in the end, it was the fact that his friends were staying at the *lycée* that persuaded him.

*

At the end of the day's classes, Steve hung around near the door to the block where first year science classes were held. A stream of students flowed out, forming pools between the plain white buildings and under the covered walkways between them. Steve glimpsed Nathalie, distinctive with her streak of red hair. She was surrounded by other girls in jeans and tops of various colours and youths in tight black trousers. For a while, Steve watched, hesitating to approach her among friends. He could imagine the laughter. However, the stream of students separated into rivulets and Nathalie stopped to chat to Amélie by one of the columns supporting the roof of the walkway. Steve strolled to meet them.

"I thought you were in the second year," Nathalie said. "What are you doing here?"

Steve realised he hadn't worked out what to say to her. "I wondered how you were getting on. I could show you round."

Nathalie laughed. "I can find my way, thanks." She draped her arm over Amélie's shoulder. "I've got mates. And my brother was here."

Two girls detached themselves from the stream flowing past and called out. "Are you coming with us?"

105

"See you." Amélie said and wandered off to join them. Nathalie hesitated. "I'll come in a bit."

Encouraged by her decision to stay, Steve pressed on. "I could help you with English homework." He'd discovered, even at *collége*, that he could trade his knowledge of the language for help with other subjects.

Nathalie stood with her head tipped to one side, considering him. "I reckon I know your Maman."

His mouth drooped open for a moment. "You never."

"She works for my Papa. He's chef at Le Pont restaurant."

Steve remembered his mother telling him about the restaurant and the people she'd met there. The chef was called François and sounded stern.

"You don't look much like your Maman," Nathalie said.

Steve shook his head. "People say I look more like Papa. D'you look like your Maman? She must have been pretty."

Nathalie laughed, and tossed her dark hair. "You're talking bullshit." She moved closer and whispered in his ear. "We could give each other bits of gossip about our parents. That'd be fun."

It wasn't Steve's idea of fun, but he nodded. Nathalie's closeness tempted him to touch her, so he stroked the red streak in her hair. "Why red?"

She laughed. "I like it."

"So do I," he said, letting his hand stray onto her slim neck under her ear with its gold stud.

"I used to think you were an idiot."

He thought about the incident when he nearly dropped the peaches. "No."

"No, you're quite nice really."

He drew encouragement from this and let his hand stray further.

"Nathalie. Are you coming?" yelled Amélie, on her way to the school gate.

"Gotta go." She started walking towards her friends, then turned back towards him. " See you."

*

Mushroom picking at the Ricaud's was a traditional autumn activity. Steve wasn't interested in mushrooms but he liked walking in the woods, looking for birds and deer, so on Sunday he arrived at the Ricaud's house with binoculars and a notebook. For a while, he stood outside the barn watching André demonstrating the controls of his scooter. A small white van drove into the farmyard and Nathalie stepped out, wearing jeans and a long sleeved purple top. Steve stared in surprise, until she was followed by a tall, dark-haired man. This must be her father, the chef. Nathalie smiled at Steve and André but made no move towards them.

A moment later, Georges Ricaud emerged from the house with his brown and white dog, followed by Amélie, carrying a collection of flat baskets. Steve and André wandered over to the group by the door and the dog trotted round, wagging her tail. Georges, who was chatting to Nathalie's father, turned towards Steve and introduced them.

"Are you Alison Delaney's son?" asked François, giving Steve's hand a firm grip.

"Yes."

He smiled. "I think she would like some wild mushrooms. If

you don't know which ones to pick, ask me."

"Thanks." Despite his mother's descriptions, François seemed friendly.

Before the party started, Amélie walked round the group, presenting everyone with baskets. She smiled at Steve. "You can keep anything you pick," she told him. "That's Papa's rule."

They followed a track into the wood behind the Ricaud's house. The path became stony as the ground rose between trees and an undergrowth of bushes. It was a bright morning, with a fronding of cloud and the only signs of autumn were berries on hawthorns, nuts on hazels and a few withered leaves among the oaks' heavy foliage. From time to time, the dog stopped and dug among tree roots but came when Georges called. Steve wanted to join Nathalie but found himself with the men, as the girls trailed behind, chatting.

Georges stopped and pointed to a line of cloven hoof prints in mud beside the path. "Deer. Recent."

François nodded. "If you shoot a few, can I have some meat for Le Pont?"

"Of course."

"It's a while since my brother shot any *sangliers* on his farm."

"I've never seen wild boar," said Steve. He'd heard stories about them and wanted to know which to believe. Some people said they were dangerous but the young ones looked cute: stripy with curly tails.

Georges smiled. "Would you want to shoot them?"

Steve hesitated. He had mixed views on the subject of shooting but wasn't going to discuss them in this company.

François looked at him, thoughtful. "They cause a lot of damage. And the meat is good."

Steve nodded.

The group moved on but the pause had enabled the girls to catch up. Steve saw André chatting to Nathalie and wanted to stop his friend monopolising her. He wandered over to join them.

"Are you interested in mushrooms?" asked Nathalie.

"Not really." He glanced at her. "I thought you might be here."

She laughed. "Liar. I only decided to come yesterday. I just wanted to see Amélie."

Her closeness encouraged him to try to touch her but she walked away and rejoined Amélie. From time to time, Georges and François left the path and scuffed among the undergrowth of brambles and dead leaves. The dog joined them, wagging her tail and sniffing. After a while, Georges bent to pick something.

He held up a mushroom with a thick white stalk and brown cap."*cèpes*."

Everyone joined the search under a group of oaks. After a few minutes, Steve found a *cèpe* nestling among leaves, eased the mushroom out of the soil and put it in his basket. He found two more as the group neared the highest point of the hill. As he walked, he heard something pecking among the trees and moved in the direction of the sound. At last he saw a green woodpecker on the trunk of an old pine. He took out his binoculars and watched the bird for a while.

By the time it flew off, most of the group had moved on but Nathalie was standing, with her hand on a tree trunk, a few metres away.

"What were you looking at?"she asked, as he approached.

"A woodpecker." If she was on her own maybe he could kiss her.

"Why do you like them?"

"They're interesting. But I like you better." He sneaked an arm round her waist and, this time, she didn't move.

She smiled. "You're funny."

"But do you like me?"

"Perhaps."

She was very close now, so he bent his head and tried to kiss her. Their lips met, slipped sidewards and met again. Aware his attempts to kiss were awkward, he was afraid she might think him childish.

"Nathalie, Steve!" Georges called from somewhere in the wood.

"We must go. Papa will be cross." She wriggled free.

"Your Papa seemed OK."

Nathalie pouted. "He thinks I'm still a child."

As Steve rejoined the group, François was standing under an oak tree with a basket full of mushrooms. Steve made a mental note to be careful with Nathalie while her father was present. Maybe it would be safer to look for her at school, when he got the opportunity.

Chapter 13

Brian ambled out of the house to visit a jumble-sale in the village. Normally he wouldn't have bothered but Alison thought he should go. The event was raising funds for a local school, and many of their neighbours would be there. Besides, it was a pleasant day, bright with a breeze that ruffled the leaves of the Virginia Creeper trailing over the hedge in their front garden. Brian felt ill at ease, uncertain of his status in his own home. His plum picking hadn't been appreciated, and his attempt to cycle had led to a row with Steve. He'd tried to repair the damage by jamming the plums he'd picked, but left some burnt sugar at the bottom of the pan. Steve had laughed and Alison insisted he cleaned it up.

As Brian reached the end of the drive, he found a tape stretching across the road, preventing cars from driving towards the Mairie. The triangle of grass behind the church had disappeared under a muddle of parked cars. Red notices announcing *Vide-Grenier, St Thomas* were attached to every lamp post, flapping occasionally in the breeze. Groups of people loitered around a straggle of stalls along the road. Alison was talking to a neighbour, Agnès Gomez, by a stall near the church. It would be polite to go and see what the old lady had on offer.

The road sloped steeply, giving Agnès a problem with her stall. Although one table leg was propped to give a flat surface, cutlery and table mats were sliding downhill. Agnès kept rearranging them, whilst conducting a conversation with Alison. Something about a niece which didn't interest Brian. Agnès was

111

making an attempt to be smart, in a skirt and white blouse, instead of her usual shapeless trousers. He looked through her wares, and found them uninspiring. There were piles of old-fashioned cardigans and skirts, a set of flowery plates, some of which were chipped, and a selection of kitchen utensils. He spent a few moments pretending to examine a mixing bowl before moving on.

On the way towards the Mairie, Brian passed a stall stocked with old computers and books, and another where two young women were displaying woven baskets. He wondered if he and Alison should have taken a stall, but they had amassed little during their two years in France. They had sold everything they could from their house in England before they left. He turned into the square in front of the Mairie and wandered past the stalls arranged round the edge. Even in the September sunshine, the effect was scruffy and moth-eaten.

As Brian passed a stall cluttered with household items, including bowls, vases and cutlery, he noticed something interesting. A brass carriage clock. He stopped and stared, guessing it was old. Small but elegant, with a hinged carrying handle and Roman numerals. The old man sitting behind the stall watched him, a cigarette drooping from his lips. An idea occurred to Brian. The clock had probably been left in some corner of an old house for years, and the seller might have little sense of its worth. If he could buy it cheaply and resell at a profit, it would earn them a little money.

"Does this clock work?" he asked.

The old man fumbled in a box of oddments and found a key. Once he'd wound up the clock and set the hands, it began ticking.

"How much?"

The stall holder gazed at him, assessing how much he would pay. "Thirty Euros."

"Twenty," said Brian, keen to drive the price down.

The old man threw his cigarette stub on the ground. "Twenty five."

"OK."

Brian drew out a couple of crumpled notes, handed them over and walked off with the clock. He thought he might have a bargain and his mind was full of ideas. France had hundreds of sales of jumble and second-hand goods – *vides-greniers* and *brocantes*. If he could pick up bargains and make a profit, he'd stumbled on the basis for a business.

At the war memorial in front of the church, he met Alison. Her shopping bag looked empty and he guessed she'd only visited the stalls to demonstrate solidarity with their neighbours.

"What have you got there?" she asked, her voice lifting in surprise.

"I bought this clock. It might be worth something."

She held out her hand and he passed her the clock. "What are you going to do with it?"

He smiled, thinking she'd failed to spot the opportunity that had occurred to him. "Sell it, of course."

She turned it over and looked at the base. "What did you pay for it?"

"Twenty five Euros, and I reckon it's a bargain. It looks old."

"But we don't know anything about clocks." She pursed her lips in a way he always found annoying.

"I can find out." Brian wondered if Carrie might know about clocks. "I'll go to the English library and see if they've got anything useful."

"If you can't sell it, that's twenty five Euros we can't afford."

"Give me a chance," he said. "You need to be more positive."

"Well, I'll wait and see."

As they walked back to the house, Brian felt a niggling resentment. Alison was growing sceptical about his ideas: trying to dismiss them without giving him a chance to prove they could work. In the past, she would have given a more sympathetic hearing. He accepted his idea of working as a tutor hadn't been properly thought out, so he needed to do his research first if he was going to try to sell the clock. It would give him an excuse to see Carrie again. She might be more receptive than Alison.

*

When Brian arrived in Beaumont he was in a cheerful mood. He'd managed to scrounge a lift from old Albert Couzineau, who was visiting relatives, and told Alison he was going to borrow a book about antiques from the English library. It was unnecessary to add that, on Tuesday morning, Carrie worked there. Not that he needed to be secretive about his meetings with Carrie, because there was nothing between them except friendship. But Alison might be suspicious and he didn't want to provide her with material for yet another row.

Seeing Carrie in the library cheered him further. She was sitting at the desk, the light through the blue blinds giving her silver earrings a sheen. An old woman with silver hair was talking to her about the merits of various romantic novels. Brian turned aside and looked at the notices pinned on a board on the wall. Although some concerned the rules of the library, there were flyers giving details of trips to places of interest and a new series of French conversation classes.

"Sold any paintings?" he asked Carrie, once the old woman had wandered to the rows of shelving.

"Quite a few. How's the novel getting on?"

Reluctant to admit he'd made no progress, Brian changed the subject. "Actually, I came because I saw an old clock at a *vide grenier* the other day. Snapped it up. I thought it might be worth a bit. I wondered if you'd got any books on antiques."

"Several." She rose and led Brian to two rows of shelving, laden with books on art and crafts. He stood beside her, aware of the musky fragrance she wore, and of her hair touching his cheek. In this quiet place, she was flamboyant in her orange blouse and cinnamon coloured skirt with mirror work round the hem.

She took down a book and turned the pages. "Here are the clocks."

He took his time looking through the illustrations, enjoying her closeness. "It might be one of these," he said, pointing to one of the simpler carriage clocks.

"Well, why don't you borrow this book and check it out?" Carrie returned to the desk with the book under her arm.

As she stamped the book, Brian lingered, thinking of a way to prolong the conversation. "Do you know anything about antique dealers round here?"

She laughed. "Do you think you can make some money from it?"

He shrugged as if it was unimportant. "It might be possible."

"What happened to the *chambre d'hôte*? I thought that was going to be your source of income."

"It's taking a while." He sensed a sharpness in Carrie's question and knew it wouldn't be easy to fool her. It would be better to avoid any mention of the Mayor's visit. As the old woman returned to the desk, with a couple of books in bright covers, Brian stepped aside. Almost glad of the interruption, he

115

leafed through the antiques book, took his glasses off and polished them.

Once the old woman had left the library, Carrie looked at Brian again. "You could try the shop selling antiques and *brocante*, on the road to Castelnau. I've bought frames from them on occasion." She smiled. "Good luck with your antiques."

"I think selling antiques would suit me." Reluctant to admit he was losing ground with Carrie, he decided to make another attempt to see her outside the library. "Can I offer you a coffee? Or something stronger?"

She shook her head, sending her earrings swinging. "Sorry, I've promised to stay until twelve. And I shan't be doing this job much longer. I need to spend more time on my painting."

Brian sighed. "When can I see you again, then?"

"You can ring me. But please don't just turn up while I'm painting."

He picked up his book and left, his enthusiasm diluted by frustration. Although he'd found some information for his researches, Carrie was closing down his opportunities to see her. Maybe, when it came to dealing with women, he was losing his touch. Getting old. It was possible Carrie meant what she said and needed some quiet time to paint. However, he suspected she'd been so hurt by her previous encounters with men that she was distrustful of the whole sex. And he supposed he hadn't much to offer, being married and short of money. It grated that her paintings were selling, while his novel writing had got nowhere. Brian accepted that he needed to put more money in his pocket before he did anything else. However, he had time to kill before meeting Albert for the journey home, and the Café des Voyageurs beckoned.

*

The shop selling *Brocante et Antiquités* was housed in an old limestone barn. Evidence that some people managed to renovate their barns. Brian opened one of two big doors, carrying his precious clock wrapped in tissue paper, and stepped into a large show room, full of furniture, china and ornaments, carefully displayed to best effect. There were groups of matching chairs and tables in polished wood, and ornate chests of drawers, set with silver dishes, laid out as if they were ready for use. A teddy bear rested on a settee, and two antique bicycles leant against the nearest wall.

He moved round the room carefully, so as not to risk damaging anything. A woman who might have been in her sixties appeared from a doorway and walked towards him. Her grey hair was fastened into a chignon, and she wore a navy dress, with a gold chain at the neck and several rings.

"Can I help you, Monsieur?" Her thin lips were pressed into a smile that wasn't reflected in her eyes.

Brian assumed as much confidence as he could, as he unwrapped his clock, and placed it on one of the polished tables. "I'm interested in selling this carriage clock. It's in good condition."

The old woman looked him up and down, as if trying to place him in some category of seller. At last, she picked up the clock with red nailed fingers. "Let me look."

She clicked across the room in high heels to an adjoining office. Brian followed her and stood opposite as she sat at a desk. It was obvious that she regarded him as not important enough to be invited to sit down. Although Brian liked to think of himself as a ladies' man, he found it difficult to deal with women in positions of authority. He jammed his hands in his pockets and tried to disguise his resentment. He'd asked a legitimate question and didn't expect to be treated like a servant. She might be the owner of a successful antique business, but he was a man of intelligence and some knowledge of the world.

The woman took out an eyeglass and examined the clock, turning it over and running her finger over the brass case. "It's from the second half of the nineteenth century, and not of particular interest. I'll give you fifty Euros for it."

Brian hesitated. Although he'd researched French carriage clocks, he wasn't qualified to query a professional judgement. But he wasn't accepting this offer without question, and reached out his hand to take the clock. "I'll take it somewhere else."

The old woman looked at him with cold eyes. "I'll go as high as seventy Euros. Not more than that."

"Very well," said Brian, reflecting that he'd still make a decent profit at that price.

The woman counted out a pile of notes. As Brian walked out, he felt her eyes follow him all the way to the door. He was fuming at the contempt her manner indicated. She was a snobbish bitch. Although she might be able to behave like an authority on antiques here in rural France, he doubted whether she'd survive in Paris, or London. He amused himself thinking that a real London antiques expert would make her look like a beginner.

All the same, he'd succeeded in selling the carriage clock and had made forty five Euros on the deal. If he could do some more research, find out what was valuable, and buy a few more promising items, he could make some money. He thought of Alison, working ridiculous hours in Le Pont restaurant. He would show her there were better and easier ways to earn a living.

Chapter 14

The walk along the riverside became a welcome part of Alison's day at Le Pont. If she needed shops or the bank, she walked into the centre of Caillac, but she preferred the tranquillity of the roadway leading to the slipway. Sometimes she saw the florist, Yvonne Mathieu, who would stop potting plants or arranging flowers and have a chat. Other days she continued to the slipway. During the week there was little activity among the boats moored by the river. However on Saturday, she saw a man in a leather jerkin and waders reverse a land rover with a trailer down the slipway. It looked as if he was ready to take a boat out of the water.

As she watched, François strolled from the direction of Le Pont. Alison felt sure he was seeking out her company. "Do you like boats?" he asked.

Remembering her childhood, Alison smiled. "When I was a girl, I lived near the coast. I used to go sailing with my family. That's one thing I miss here – the sea."

François turned towards her. "So why did you come here?"

A man in jeans and a jersey, who might have been a boat owner, unhitched a small cruiser from a ring on the river wall. He walked past them, keeping close to the water's edge and drawing the boat until it floated above the slipway.

"I like rural France as well." Alison wondered how to explain the decision. It might seem a whim to François, indeed the *chambre d'hôte* project had come to seem ill advised to her. "I don't much like cities but I worked in London for years. I was glad to leave."

"I've always lived near the Lot. Except the two years I spent in Toulouse, training. My father had a farm on the hills north of Caillac."

"But you didn't want to be a farmer?" asked Alison.

The man in a jerkin waded into the river, until the water was near the top of his waders and started securing the boat to the trailer.

François shook his head. "I always knew that my brother René would get the farm. My father left me money and I used it to buy the restaurant. He used to grow everything – wheat, plums, grapes, vegetables. And he kept cows and ducks. A lot of work for a small farm. René specialises in growing plums and keeping ducks. And he's got a truffle wood. He sometimes he gives me truffles." He smiled. "Have you tried truffles?"

"No, they're too expensive."

"I must give you some of our truffle sauce."

The two men finished tying the boat to the trailer. The man in the jerkin climbed into the land rover and pulled the boat clear of the water. Once the boat had reached the top of the slope, the two men stood beside it chatting. It looked as if the activity was over.

"I love cooking, but there are times I wished..." François sighed. "I promised to show Pierre how to bone duck."

On returning to the restaurant, Alison didn't need to start work immediately, so she ambled to her place by the sink. François was boning a duck, his fingers moving with delicacy and speed. He handed the knife to Pierre, patiently corrected and encouraged his efforts. As preparation for the evening meal started in earnest, Pierre started his usual tasks of chopping vegetables and laying out garnishes at the plating table. Gérard returned to the kitchen and stood at one of the hobs. He was sautéing something that gave off an earthy fragrance.

As Gérard stirred, François looked up, smiled at Alison and moved to the hob. "Sauce aux truffes. Come and see. You only use a little truffle. They have an intense taste." François dipped a spoon in the mixture. "Taste it." He raised a spoonful of sauce and slipped it between her lips.

Steam rose from the pan and the rich taste of the mushrooms lingered in Alison's mouth. Her closeness to François gave her a sudden desire to feel his hands caressing her. They were strong hands, capable of cleaving meat, but also of great delicacy. She took a step back, flustered. "It's delicious."

Gérard gave Alison a smile that was almost a leer as she returned to her place by the sink, confused. She drew on her rubber gloves and turned on the tap, glad of the clouds of steam, which hid her embarrassment from others. But not from herself.

***

When the phone rang, Brian was sitting in the writer's room, with a bottle of Armagnac and a page of notes about ways to make money selling antiques. He padded down the stairs to take the call in the living room. The autumn evenings were shortening, so he turned the lights on, sat at the corner desk and tried to block his ears to the music rumbling out of Steve's room.

Tim's voice. "It's a while since I heard from you. How are you doing?"

Brian was determined to be positive. "We're fine. Alison's out at the moment. She's got a job in a restaurant."

"In a restaurant? That's not her usual line."

Hearing the surprise in Tim's voice, Brian invented. "She

wanted to get out of the house, do something different. And there aren't many jobs going round here." There was some truth in both statements. In his experience, it was bad for anyone to be stuck in the house for too long.

There was a pause at the end of the line. "And what about your renovation work?"

Brian took his glasses off, polished them and put them back. "We're having a few problems. This is France. Everything takes a long time."

"Oh. What kind of problems?" There was a suspicious tone in Tim's voice.

"French bureaucracy is a nightmare. There are so many regulations and they want everything in triplicate." This was also more or less true.

" We were hoping to come and see you in mid October. Is that still OK?"

Brian looked round the room: at the sand coloured armchairs, the crack in the wall which had been mended. It was passable. "Yes, that's fine. There's plenty of space. We can certainly put you up."

Tim sounded relieved. "We'll be glad to see you. We can talk about things then."

Brian padded into the kitchen to find a bottle of wine, and sat at the table. A muddle of plates, knives and forks remained to be washed after the makeshift meal he and Steve had eaten. They hadn't spoken much. Brian thought about Tim and Helen. What would they say on arriving at the house and finding progress stalled? He loathed Helen, who clearly regarded him as a threat to her family, and found Tim's aura of confident businessman irritating. They would be angry when they discovered the money they'd lent towards the renovation work had gone. He'd used it to pay a few bills and avoid running up an unauthorised overdraft. There would be some way to repay the loan, he was sure of that. The idea of selling antiques appealed, but his plans weren't ready yet.

He knew he would have to give Alison an account of the phone call, so he sat in the kitchen, drinking and smoking the occasional cigarette. He was on his second bottle of wine by the time Steve wandered in, saying nothing. "Aren't you talking to me?" asked Brian.

"I wish you wouldn't drink all the time." Steve opened the fridge freezer and took out a can of Coca Cola.

"I don't know how many times I've told you. You've got no business telling me what to do."

"I have to live in this house." Steve walked out of the kitchen and slammed the door.

By the time he heard the car on the drive Brian's head was on the table. As Alison entered, he put his glasses on and struggled to focus his eyes on her face. He knew there was something he needed to tell her, but it took him a moment to remember what. "Tim rang," he said eventually. "He's coming over in mid October."

Alison started piling up plates and cutlery, then drew up a chair and sat down. "I've no idea what we're going to say to Tim. It'll be difficult..."

"We'll tell him we'll pay him back as soon as we can. Of course we will. It's just a matter of time."

"I don't see where we're going to get the money." She picked up one of the bottles on the table, turned it upside down and watched the drips. Evidence of his failings.

"We'll find a way. I could sell antiques. It might take a bit of research and some investment..."

" We're never going to make enough selling antiques to pay our debts. How much do we owe, anyway? I don't even know where you keep the papers."

Brian groaned, took his glasses off again and laid them on the table. "Not now."

"I insist."

He was surprised by her determination. It seemed her experience of being the breadwinner was changing her, making her more determined. He couldn't be bothered to fight any longer. " They're upstairs in the writer's room. Fat lot of good it will do you."

***

On Monday morning, Alison climbed the stairs to the writer's room and sat at the desk. This was Brian's domain and she'd ceased to move his papers, simply dusting round them. She knew there were files of notes and drafts of his novel. There might be other things hidden, including the financial papers she was determined to find. She couldn't accept his view of their money problems without argument, as that was the reaction of a woman who didn't think for herself. Instead she wanted to form her own judgement. It was important to keep Steve out of the discussion, so she'd waited until he was at school. She even entrusted Brian with the task of going shopping, although she knew he'd return with more wine than she could afford.

Under one of the files, Alison found a plain buff folder. When she opened it, a pile of bills and letters fell out. As she leafed through them, she felt a growing horror at the red messages: "Final Demand. We will commence legal action". For some time she sat at the desk with her head in her hands. How would she make sense of it all? How would she deal with so much debt?

Her parents had brought her up wary of debt. She could imagine her father's rage if he saw the piles of unpaid bills on the desk. He had read her the advice of Wilkins Micawber from *David Copperfield.* "'Annual income twenty pounds, annual expenditure nineteen nineteen and six, result happiness. Annual income twenty pounds, annual expenditure twenty pounds ought and six, result misery.'" Although she'd taken little note of words from a nineteenth century novel at the time, they were returning to haunt her.

She shook herself, fumbled in the desk drawer for a calculator and sorted the bills into categories. As she read through letters from banks, she found gaps in payments towards their mortgage and other loans she couldn't begin to repay. The harder she tried to calculate the total, the more confusing the picture became. What interest rates were they paying? Where the demands from creditors were in pounds, how could she convert them to Euros? Despite her uncertainties, she was sure of one thing: they needed to try to pay something towards the mortgage. She didn't want to lose the house.

Chapter 15

Alison hurried in through the kitchen door of Le Pont and closed her umbrella. The end of September had brought rain, which merged puddles on the roadway outside into pools, and reduced the bridge to a darker shape in mist. Having stowed the umbrella and shaken her coat in the staff cloakroom, she stood in the hall, midway between the back door and the stairs to the restaurant. Through the small pane of glass in the office door she could see François working at his desk. The hall was not a pleasant place to loiter, with its plain plastered walls, cold stone floor and naked light bulbs. However she wondered if she could face the others in the bar.

She'd spent much of Monday working through the papers that had been lying hidden in the writer's room. The extent of the debts she'd uncovered horrified her. At the first opportunity, she'd been to the bank to make a transfer of money to England to make a payment on the mortgage. Although she'd got together as much as she could afford, she knew it wasn't enough. She could save as much as possible on the housekeeping, but the hole in their finances would keep growing. And she was concerned about her brother's visit. Although she would be glad to see Tim, she worried what his reaction would be when he realised the extent of their problem. Helen might be sharper.

François emerged from the office. "You must have got very wet."

"I only went to the bank." Alison was conscious that her shoes were leaving wet marks on the flagstones.

"Why not go and sit in the bar?"

She stood in the middle of the hall, wondering how to explain her indecision.

"Is something wrong?"

"I don't feel like chatting." She looked down at her wet feet.

He studied her with concern. "Can you tell me what's happened?"

"I don't know if it would make sense to you because..." Alison stopped, aware of a growing desire to tell François everything. There were few people in whom she could confide and he offered a combination of reliability and kindness.

"Let's go in the office. Everyone can see you here." He laid a hand on Alison's shoulder, and ushered her into the little room, which she hadn't entered since her interview. There seemed to be more dust on the filing cabinets and desk than before. She sat on the battered chair.

François stood beside her, his hand still on her shoulder. "What wouldn't make sense to me?"

"I thought I was doing well, earning money for the three of us at home. But I hadn't realised how much debt we've got, and now my brother's coming to see us..." Her voice wavered.

"Why is your brother coming a problem?" he asked, frowning.

"I borrowed money from him. And from banks. We thought we could renovate our barns as a *chambre d'hôte*. But then the Mayor said no, we couldn't do it. And we can't pay Tim back."

" That's bad. But is there no one who can help? What about your husband ? Doesn't he work?"

Alison hesitated. She knew that her marriage to Brian was disintegrating, but felt reluctant to reveal the extent of her disillusion. It felt like a betrayal, especially as she found François attractive. "Brian drinks too much. He thinks he has good ideas but they don't work out."

"I'm sorry." François stroked her hair, bent down and kissed the back of her neck where the hair curled.

She drew away, confused. Although she enjoyed his touch, this wasn't the time or place. "I shouldn't have bothered you with my problems."

"I'd like to help but... " He took a step back and stood hesitant for several moments. "Usually in October, I close Le Pont on Tuesdays. There isn't the demand."

Alison started working out what her income would be if she was only working four days a week.

"But you could do some simple preparation. I'd pay you more per hour and it would be good for Pierre to help Gérard with sauces."

"That would be helpful. But I'm not asking for special treatment." She rose, wondering about the advances he'd made to her. He hadn't seemed the sort of man who took advantage of his staff. Perhaps the gesture had meant more. But she didn't want to feel obliged to him.

He shook his head. "You're a good worker. And I know you cook at home. I'm sure I can trust you with chopping vegetables."

"Of course. Thank you." Alison left the office and climbed the steps to the restaurant. All she had gained was a sympathetic listener. She was no nearer resolving the problem of the family's debts, and she'd learnt something which complicated her position further. The attraction between her and François was mutual.

***

Rugby wasn't Steve's favourite game. A persistent rain was falling and he ambled onto the pitch without enthusiasm. When play started, the ball was kicked into the other half of the pitch and he trotted after the forwards. It was some minutes before the opposing pack hurtled in his direction and Steve hurried towards the action. A scrum formed with André deep in the middle, the ball was cleared and kicked in his direction. Steve made a grab for it and ran. Usually, he was a good runner but the muddy ground slowed him and a tackle sent him flying. He picked himself up in time to see a try by the opposing side. However, the forwards from his team were soon back at the other end of the pitch. After a try by Steve's side, the opposing forwards gained possession, there was a ruck and Steve caught the cleared ball. He evaded the opposition long enough to run down the pitch and kick the ball to a team member, who scrambled over the line. A series of scrums followed, in which André played a key part, and at the final whistle Steve's team had won by a good margin. Steve rushed to André, who stood in the middle of the pitch steaming and grinning, and flung a muddy arm over his shoulder.

At the end of the game the teams trudged back to the changing rooms covered in mud. To Steve's surprise, Nathalie was standing under the covered walkway near the door to the main building. He felt a moment of delight, hoping she was waiting for him, only for it to fade as André trotted over to her. She slipped a slim arm round his muddy waist and gave him a squeeze. Steve watched with a sense of betrayal as they ambled into the main building together.

In the changing room, Steve reached the rows of metal lockers. André was standing by his, covered in mud and sweat, and carrying a towel and a bundle of clothes.

"What's going on between you and Nathalie?" asked Steve, taking a step towards him.

André slammed his locker. "We're friends."

"What kind of friend?"

"What's that to you?"

"Have you been snogging her?"

André's round face flushed. "Have you?"

"Why should you have the prettiest girl?"

"What you getting at?"

For a minute, the two friends stood chest to chest. Although André was a head taller, as well as broader, Steve was reluctant to give way. He wasn't going to lose Nathalie without a struggle.

A member of the opposing team barged past on his way along the line of lockers, stopped and slapped André on the shoulder. "Well played."

André smiled and the tension broke. Steve opened his locker, grabbed his clothes and made for the showers. As he stood under a stream of warm water, he argued with himself. André was a good friend but, if he was after Nathalie, it meant trouble. The Ricauds had known the Allomberts for ages and André might simply be on friendly terms with Nathalie. But why didn't he say so? Steve had kissed her and the memory of her soft body against his filled him with longing. Still angry and confused, Steve rubbed himself down, gathered up his clothes and left the changing rooms.

By the time he unlocked his bike, the rain had stopped, the clouds had become ragged fragments and afternoon sunshine glinted on puddles. Glad to be going home in the dry, Steve cycled out of the gate. Groups of girls and guys were walking along a street lined by suburban houses, which led from the school. As he neared the junction with the main road, he spotted a girl carrying a red umbrella. Nathalie.

He stopped beside her and dismounted. "Are you going home? I'll walk with you."

"If you like." She folded the umbrella and walked beside him. "Do you always go to school on that bike?"

He nodded, then seeing the surprise in her eyes, he boasted a little. "It's not difficult if you're fit."

She laughed. "Perhaps you like getting wet."

"Not really." Steve grinned, then lapsed into silence. He was wondering how to raise the subject of the rugby game and her relationship with André. It was bothering him and would go on doing so until he got an answer. If André wasn't prepared to tell him the truth, he'd have to ask Nathalie.

They turned into the main road, which climbed towards the centre of Caillac. In the distance, the church spire rose above its surroundings. To remain close to Nathalie, Steve pushed his bike carefully between school students standing and wandering around on the pavement. Nathalie waved at a group of girls loitering under a plane tree. Realising she might want to stop and chat, he decided to seize the opportunity. "What were you saying to André?"

"André?" She stopped and looked at him. "Why are you talking about André?"

"You were cuddling up to him after the rugby." He couldn't prevent an accusing tone creeping into his voice.

"You're jealous." There was laughter in her eyes.

"Do you like him better than me?" He realised he'd confirmed her suspicion but didn't care.

"André's an old friend." She moved close and kissed him briefly on the lips. "But I like you in a different way."

Steve enfolded her in his arms for a while, drawing her close and kissing her neck.

There was a yell from one of the other girls and Nathalie drew away. "I'm going to join my friends. I'll see you at school."

Steve watched her walking away, school bag in one hand and umbrella in the other. He could hardly take his eyes off her. Everything about her entranced him: her hair, her face, her walk, her laugh. Was this love?

*

When the phone rang later that evening, Steve was inclined to let Dad answer it. He was sitting in his room drawing a picture of the jackdaws which roosted near the château. It was easy enough to show them sitting on branches, but not to catch them in flight. He liked the way they flew: tumbling and turning as if for fun. In theory he was supposed to be doing English homework but could hurry through that. Being English in a French school had some advantages. He'd finish his sketch first.

After the phone had rung a couple of times and Dad hadn't come downstairs, Steve wandered into the living room and picked it up.

Gran's voice. "Is that Brian?"

"No, Gran, it's me, Steve."

"Oh, I was hoping to talk to your mother. Is she in?" There was something whiny about Gran's tone. Steve wondered if she was ill, as she was very old.

"She's at work. She doesn't come in 'til about midnight." Steve hadn't seen Gran since he left for France but he'd enjoyed her company when he was younger. He remembered her taking him on a trip to the Crystal Palace, where he'd roamed round the gardens, coming face to face with dinosaurs. When he'd complained they weren't like the pictures he'd seen in books, Gran had explained that they'd been made by the Victorians, who were just discovering dinosaurs and made mistakes.

"I remember now," said Gran. "She said she was cooking or something."

"She's washing up in a restaurant."

"Washing up? Why's she doing such a menial job?"

"We need the money." He'd noticed the disapproval in Gran's voice and wondered if he'd said the wrong thing. He wasn't good at being diplomatic, preferring to say what he thought. Anyway he saw no reason to lie to Gran about Mum's work. It might be menial but he respected her for working.

"What for? I can't believe you're short of food. Not in France."

An idea occurred to him. Since Gran had given him the money for his camera, she might be prepared to pay for other things he needed. "We've got enough food and stuff. But I could do with a scooter to get to school and we can't afford it."

"A scooter? Are you old enough?"

"I'm sixteen," he protested.

Steve heard a heavy footstep on the stairs. His Dad wandered over and looked at him suspiciously. "Who are you talking to?" he demanded.

" D'you want to talk to Dad, Gran?"

"Not particularly. I'd rather talk to you."

Steve recognised the snub in this reply and turned to his father, embarrassed. "I was only chatting."

Dad turned a darker shade of red and turned away. "All right. I know when I'm not wanted. I was never good enough for her daughter."

Steve watched his father lumber back upstairs, wondering

133

whether to pity or despise him.

"How are you doing at school?" asked Gran.

"Fine. And I'm doing a lot of wildlife drawings. I'm really grateful for the camera you gave me."

"I'm glad it's been useful. And I might be able to send some money for you to get a scooter. Though I'd want to talk to your Mum first."

"Oh thanks Gran. That'd be great. I'll ask Mum to ring you."

When Steve put the phone down, he smiled. Not only might he get the scooter he wanted, but he'd also won another small battle with Dad.

Chapter 16

A few days later, Alison set out to walk to the bank again because they'd rejected a direct debit. In her concern to make payments toward the mortgage, she'd left herself short of money for the water bill. She'd gathered together as much cash as she could, but trudged in a melancholy mood. The rain had stopped but a brisk wind was driving the surface of the river into crests, and making the boats' radio aerials whistle. She'd added a black jacket to black trousers and a cream blouse. Maybe she was choosing her clothes with more thought now she knew François was looking at her.

As she approached the bridge, she heard footsteps and looked round to see him, walking from the restaurant with long strides. His only concession to the weather was to pull a navy jersey over his usual jeans. As he slowed his pace to walk beside her, she smiled, glad of his company. The memory of the kiss he'd planted on the back of her neck lingered in her mind.

"Going shopping?" he asked.

She shook her head. "I'm still having trouble with the bank."

"Have you tried asking at the Mairie? They can be helpful sometimes."

"You should have heard what Brian said about the Mayor of St. Thomas." Despite herself, Alison smiled a little, as she decided not to translate Brian's rude English.

François smiled. "You need to be friends with your Mayor."

Cultivating relationships, that was how things were done here. Although she knew François was fair in dealing with his staff, she could imagine him treating the local Mayor to an occasional free meal in Le Pont. Brian had approached local officials in the wrong way.

They reached the road in front of the restaurant, crossed and turned into the main street of Caillac. As the road climbed towards the centre of town, it narrowed between old buildings, making vehicles queue and pedestrians squeeze between shop fronts and the carriageway. Alison and François edged past a van parked on the pavement.

"What did your husband do in England?" he asked, once they'd passed the obstacle.

"He worked in advertising. He did all right but he hated younger men doing better. He felt..." She tailed off, wondering how to explain Brian's disillusionment.

François shook his head. "I can't imagine a job like that. In my work, experience is an advantage. Though it's good to have a son or daughter you can pass the business on to."

Alison thought of the tensions she'd detected between François and Nathalie. "Do you mind if Nathalie doesn't want to work in a restaurant?"

"She's like her mother." He sighed.

"Simone must have been pretty." To Alison's surprise, she felt almost jealous of his missing wife.

"When I met her, yes. She was pretty and fun to be with. That was when I worked in Castelnau, before I got Le Pont. Her father owned the *boulangerie* next to the restaurant."

They stopped to wait for three old men, who stood chatting on the pavement, with cigarettes in their hands. It was a minute or two before the men finished their conversation, shook hands and went separate ways. Alison was aware of Francois's thighs in their jeans pressing against her trousers.

"It must have been a shock when she left," Alison said, as they walked on.

He nodded. "I'd been faithful, I tried to give her a decent home. But she was still unhappy. She said Caillac was boring. That I never had time for her."

Alison remembered sitting with François on the patio, talking about their families. "You said she'd found someone else."

"A man she met at her sister's. He's a lawyer. The fact he's got a big house, while we only had a flat had something to do with it."

"Money's often the source of trouble," said Alison, noticing the bitterness in Francois's voice. "Money or the lack of it." In most ways, he was was grounded: confident of his skills and his place in the community. But Simone's departure had shaken him. Alison had looked to him for consolation but maybe he needed someone too.

They reached the centre of town, where the church and the Mairie stood round a square on a rocky outcrop. She needed to cross the road to the bank, but François stopped outside the Café de La Place, which occupied one of the old half-timbered buildings at the edge of the square.

"I hadn't met anyone else I liked since Simone left. Not until I met you."

"That's nice of you." Alison blushed, aware of his dark eyes on her. "But there's Brian..."

"But can you stay with him for ever?"

"I don't know. Not for ever." The question resonated in her mind, opening frightening images of her future. In eight years

137

time, Brian would be sixty. Would he be a hopeless alcoholic? Would they be able to keep the house? If not, where would they be living? What would she be doing? Could she and Brian possibly stay together?

François gestured towards the café. "Do you want to come in for a coffee? I was going to meet my old friend Jacques. He's *le patron* here."

Alison looked inside and was tempted. A few men and one couple were sitting at tables in front of the bar. She shook her head. "I need to go to the bank. Some other time perhaps."

As she crossed the road, she thought about her admission that she couldn't stay with Brian forever. Had she given François encouragement? Did she intend that? She'd been living from day to day, counting each pay packet from Le Pont and each bill paid as a minor success. Although she realised the family was in deep financial trouble, she hadn't really asked the question how she'd be living in a few years time and whether that picture included Brian. In comparison with Brian, François seemed like a place of refuge. The idea of throwing herself in his arms was growing more and more attractive.

*

Friday was a very busy day at Le Pont. François had been delighted to get a booking from the co-operative of local plum growers, for their celebration of a successful harvest. Everything had to be right in a complex menu: starters of lobster ravioli, wild *cepes* in a cream sauce, *foie gras* in a grape salad; main courses of venison with redcurrant sauce, duckling breast in a honey and lemon sauce, salmon and fennel in puff pastry; the local *cabecou* cheese and desserts of chocolate fondant, pear tart with Armagnac and cream, and strawberry meringues. He ordered the remaining bottles of best local wine brought up from the cellar. Alison helped by preparing tomatoes for stuffing but, once the rush started, it became a giddying and complex dance and, although she was aware of François shouting at Pierre for being late with something, she didn't know what and was too busy in her own world of steam and greasy pots to care.

As the meal approached its close, the pace slackened and the chefs and waiters started to relax and chat to each other. François washed his hands, straightened his chef's whites, and left the kitchen for the restaurant.

He came back beaming. "Well done, they're all saying it was an excellent meal." He embraced or shook hands with everyone. As he approached Alison, she took off her rubber gloves to shake hands, but he kissed her on both cheeks. "You're one of the family now."

She smiled and returned to her washing up in a strange mood, where tiredness blended with happiness.

One by one, the others left and the restaurant grew quiet. Only François was still busy checking stock, as Alison took the mop and cleaned the floor.

He came over to her with a bottle of Armagnac and two glasses. "Are you in a hurry? Such a good meal deserves a celebration."

"Brian will be asleep. Steve too, I hope. But I'm tired."

"Let's go and sit in the bar."

They walked up the stairs to the restaurant and through the arch into the bar. François turned a light on and they sat by a table in a corner. She found it strange to sit in the deserted bar, which had always been busy, or at least occupied by other members of staff, when she'd been working. The glass tops of the nearby tables shone in the light, while the more distant ones receded into shadow. The result was dreamlike, increasing her sense of calm after the frenetic activity of the day.

François filled two glasses and raised his. "*Santé.*"

Alison sipped the brandy. "I'm careful about drink now. I don't want to get like Brian."

"Don't worry about Brian. You deserve a chance to relax."

She smiled at him. "So do you."

"And I like being with you. I used to think that English women were very reserved." He laid his hand on her knee.

For a moment, she thought of drawing away but changed her mind. "And I'm not reserved?"

"Maybe at first. Not now."

"I suppose I was a bit afraid of you." She remembered the nervousness of her first meeting with François. It seemed a long time ago.

He raised an eyebrow. "Not now, I hope."

She shook her head and smiled. He leaned over the table to kiss her. This time she met his lips and ran her hands through his hair. It was still thick, although there were a few grey strands among the dark ones. Close up, his eyes were lighter than she'd thought, with flecks of hazel. She and François moved apart and looked at each other for a long moment. Then they rose and embraced.

As his hands strayed down her blue top, she drew back. "François I don't know..."

"Is there no chance for me?"

She hesitated. " People might come in."

He took her hand and led her up the next flight of stairs to the flat. She knew she was taking a step she might come to regret but it no longer mattered. Life had become so confusing and worrying, the thought of some pleasure in the arms of a man she was coming to love offered too much of a temptation. The consequences could wait.

White sheets and a blue duvet lay rumpled on the double bed in François's room. The blue shutters were closed and only a single ceiling lamp lit the room, making it private and intimate. Alison kicked off her shoes and stood barefoot on the deep pile rug. As François kissed her face and neck, she peeled off her blouse, revealing white skin underneath, with a scattering of freckles between her breasts. She wished she was wearing lacy bra and pants instead of the plain ones she'd bought in a local supermarket because they were cheap. But he didn't seem to mind, running his hands over her breasts and down her body. They toppled onto the rumpled sheets, kissing and touching, entwining feet and thighs. By the time he slipped himself into her, Alison had ceased to care about her money worries.

Chapter 17

There was a sale of *brocante* in Beaumont on Sunday and Alison had agreed to go with Brian. She had her reasons. Firstly, she had a nagging awareness she had betrayed him. She didn't regret her lovemaking with François, because it had given her a new confidence. She was no longer the worn-down housewife; she was an attractive woman. Besides, she could easily argue that Brian had let her down in a variety of ways. However, he was still her husband and it was right to spend time with him. Secondly, and more practically, she wanted to make sure that he didn't spend money they couldn't afford.

They arrived in Beaumont early and tried to find a space to park near the square, but there were already vehicles on the pavement and along side streets. It took ten minutes to manoeuvre between other cars, drive out of the little town and find a place on a verge. As they walked towards the square, they saw other people heading in the same direction: middle aged women carrying baskets and old men in greasy jackets.

"Dealers," Brian said.

The sky was overcast, making the town look grey and dull, despite red and blue bunting strung between houses and lamp posts. Vans and lorries were parked round the edge of the square and men were unloading furniture and boxes. Under the plane trees stood lines of stalls, some with awnings and others that looked like little encampments, overflowing with household effects. Stallholders were arranging crockery and clothes, or standing chatting in little groups.

Together, Alison and Brian started walking along the lines of stalls looking for anything interesting. One offered an array of old guns, laid out on concrete alongside a wheelbarrow and a couple of pitchforks.

He eyed the guns. "D'you think those are any value?"

"I don't know. But I wouldn't want them in the house. "

"We can store a lot of things in the barn," he said, the light of enthusiasm in his eyes.

"Not guns."

He gave a theatrical sigh and moved on. She knew he thought of her as an obstacle to his antique selling scheme: always questioning and raising objections. But she'd seen so many of his plans start in enthusiasm, only to be abandoned or proved unworkable. This time, she wasn't going to let him risk more money than they could afford. Which wasn't much.

The next stall was surrounded with furniture. Cane chairs stood next to wooden ones with carved backs and heavy oak tables jostled with nests of small ones. Most showed the scuffs and stains of years of use. There were old mirrors with ornate wood surrounds and a couple of table lamps with brandy bottle bases. Brian examined a little polished wood desk, but shook his head when he noticed a chip in the corner.

"I'm sure we'll find something."

They came to a stall covered with crockery and glassware. There were sets of wine glasses, decanters and vases – some glass but others garish pottery. Brian stopped and looked at a couple of cut glass vases. A plump woman, sitting chatting to a friend behind the stall, stood up and pottered over.

"Are you looking for a present Monsieur? How about this one?" She pointed to a big, yellow vase.

Finding it ugly, Alison shook her head.

Brian picked up a glass pin tray, with a little figure of an owl in the centre.

"That's pretty."

He turned it over. "Lalique. That's worth having."

"Fifteen Euros," said the stall-holder.

Alison nodded and took the money out of her purse. She had set herself a limit of forty Euros and was determined to stick to it, although Brian would take years to raise any substantial profit at that rate. He'd reminded her of the saying "you have to speculate to accumulate" but she'd shaken her head.

After the woman had wrapped up the paperweight, they continued walking along the line of stalls. As they rounded a corner, a tall woman with a mass of light brown hair walked towards them. She wore a turquoise skirt and matching scarf with a tan jacket. Alison remembered her as Carrie from the French course she and Brian had attended.

Carrie smiled and stopped, depositing a shopping bag from which a large, rectangular packet protruded. "Hello Brian. It's nice to see you again, Alison."

" It seems ages since I saw you." Alison gave her a peck on both cheeks, thinking about the course. Although Carrie had struck her as charming, Brian had been more attentive to her than necessary. With her warmth and attractiveness, she was the sort of woman he might have pursued.

"Are you still interested in antiques, Brian?" asked Carrie.

"Oh yes, ones that I can afford."

Carrie winked at Alison. "I expect you have to keep him on a tight rein."

"Definitely." Although Alison smiled, she was suspicious. How many times had Brian seen Carrie since the course, and where? He hadn't mentioned meeting her again. There were times in the past when Alison had suspected him of being unfaithful, and she would have a fresh grievance against him if Carrie had become more than an acquaintance. Although Alison had lost the moral superiority, she would keep evidence of wrong doing on Brian's part. In case it proved useful.

"Carrie works in the English library sometimes," said Brian, with an attempt at nonchalance which didn't convince Alison.

"And I've got a studio up there." Carrie gestured towards the road that climbed towards the church. "I've come looking for cheap paintings. I reuse the frames."

A man lumbered in their direction, wheeling a cupboard on a trolley. They backed towards a stall whilst he passed.

Carrie patted her parcel. "Well, I've got my frames, so I'm off home. I've got a potential buyer coming this afternoon."

"Good luck with your paintings, Carrie," said Alison.

Brian smiled, nodded and moved on. A few spots of rain were beginning to fall.

"You didn't tell me you'd seen Carrie."

"I've only met her a few times."

"Is that all?"

Brian stopped by a stall selling curtains and cushion covers. "Shall we call it a day? It's raining. Though we could go to the Café des Voyageurs for some refreshments."

"No, we're going home," said Alison, taking his arm.

*

François paused with his hand on the varnished wood door of the flat. "I hope Nathalie's in bed."

Last time she'd come here, Alison had scarcely noticed her surroundings but, this time she took the opportunity to look at the living room. The cream sofa looked smart with orange cushions, but the matching carpet was stained with much use. There was an oak coffee table, marked with a ring left by a mug, and a rocking chair with a carved back, which looked as if it came from a farmhouse. Opposite the sofa stood a television and a cabinet full of old books. A pile of girl's magazines lay on the floor outside the door of the room she supposed to be Nathalie's, while the third bedroom must belong to Pierre. For a moment, Alison was surprised to see a kitchenette at the far end of the flat, beyond a half wall.

They'd come up the stairs to the flat together at the end of the evening work without hesitation. Her desire to be with François overpowered her worries and fatigue, and she walked into his bedroom with his arm round her waist. The blue duvet had been replaced by a striped one, and the sheets straightened. It pleased her that he should take the trouble to tidy the room for her. A similar feeling had made her buy new bras and pants, even though she'd still been careful not to spend too much. As he took her into his arms, she ran her hands over his shoulders and down his back.

After they'd made love, Alison lay in bed with her head on François's shoulder. There were so many things she wanted to know about his life. "It's a nice flat. Was it Simone who chose the furnishings?"

"She chose the colours and styles in the flat and the restaurant. She was interested in those things." He smiled. "You're not jealous are you?"

"Not really but I wondered why you chose me. Some of the waitresses are prettier and younger than me." The whole experience had so surprised Alison she didn't think jealousy was the right emotion. It was more disbelief. Although there had been boyfriends in her teens, since she'd met Brian, he'd been the only man in her life. There had been other men she'd found attractive, but nothing had come of those feelings.

"You intrigued me. I didn't understand why this English lady wanted to wash up in my restaurant. And you looked quite fragile but worked so hard."

"I'm not fragile really."

"I know that now." He kissed her neck at the hair line. "And I discovered you had a husband who drinks too much and doesn't work. I suppose I thought your marriage was falling apart. But I shouldn't have persuaded you..." He stopped.

"I didn't take much persuasion." That was the truth, Alison thought. She suspected her meeting with François had come at the right time, when her disillusion with Brian had reached a new intensity. It was difficult to entangle the two forces that had led her here. At the moment, she didn't want to try.

François lay back and looked at the ceiling. "I was brought up a good Catholic. We went to church every Sunday. It was the only time my parents wore their smart clothes. So they'd say I'm in a state of mortal sin."

"Do you still think that?"

"Not really. I lost whatever faith I had after my father died. He'd been ill with cancer and my mother looked after him. She died three months after he did. There just wasn't any God for me when I needed Him."

"I'm sorry," she said and planted a kiss on his forehead.

"It was hard for a while, but I've moved on. And you?"

"My parents didn't have any religion," she said, thinking they would still have disapproved of her actions. The swinging sixties had left their moral views untouched. Even her few attempts to stay out late at discos with her friends had ended after a stern reprimand from her father.

François kissed her forehead. "But you make me feel good. And it's not just sex. I suppose it's easier for me, because Simone has gone."

Alison sighed. " I still feel guilty when I'm with Brian. It doesn't make sense, because he's let me down so many times." She remembered the encounter with Carrie at the *brocante* sale, which had left her almost glad to think Brian might have another woman.

"But you still want to be with me?"

"Yes." She linked her hands round his neck. "It's just that I don't know what's going to happen to us." Although it was easy to think that her relationship with François offered some respite from her worries, it might only complicate matters. She didn't want to think about the possible consequences. Not now.

"Don't think about the future." He kissed her nose.

"I'll try not to." Alison felt it would be good to lighten the mood, talk about something else. She wondered about the little kitchenette. Having seen François working in the restaurant, she struggled to imagine him using it. But she could. The idea of preparing a meal for him appealed to her, but it had to be something he rarely made, as her skills weren't equal to his. "Perhaps I should do some cooking for you. I didn't realise you had a kitchen up here."

"It's not worth using the big kitchen for family meals."

"I could make you a curry."

"Curry's not English."

"The ones I make are."

They both laughed. A moment later, there was a noise of a door being shut in the flat.

"Nathalie's up," whispered François.

Alison slid out of bed and hurried to pull her clothes on, while he threw the bedclothes aside, dressed quickly and padded to the door. He opened it and peered into the living room, which was in darkness.

"Nobody."

"Do you think she heard?" asked Alison, putting on her shoes.

"Possibly."

"I had better go."

Alison's careless mood had gone, replaced by a deep sense of unease. If Nathalie had heard them talking and laughing, she would surely guess what was happening. At fifteen, she was knowing about sex and relationships but had little sense of responsibility. Alison could imagine Nathalie gossiping to her school friends, passing on the information her father was having an affair. Worse, Steve was one of those friends. What would happen if he found out? If Alison had thought she could keep her relationship with François secret, she'd already been proved wrong.

Chapter 18

The *lycée* common room overflowed with groups of students sitting at tables: some were reading or working at computers, while others chatted. Jackets and coats hung over chairs or lurked in heaps, along with rucksacks and sports bags. No-one wanted to venture out, because it was raining hard, streaking the windows and turning the paths between the buildings into puddles. The room was warm, steamy and full of the sounds of conversation and laughter. Steve found André playing computer games with a student with curly hair and glasses who everyone called *'Le Prof.'*

For several days, Steve and André had not spoken to each other. But Steve knew how important André's friendship was to him and hated the idea of losing it, so he had decided to make peace. He'd leafed through his wildlife sketches and chosen one of a long-eared owl, which showed its big, watchful eyes and the pattern on its plumage. Having taken it to school he'd chosen a moment when André was sitting at a desk at the beginning of a Maths lesson to hand him the sketch. "Thought you might like this."

Andre looked at the drawing and smiled. "Thanks. It's good."

"Are you still mad at me?"

"I don't think Nathalie's worth rowing about."

For a moment, Steve had thought of saying Nathalie was lovely, from the red streak in her hair to her sexy walk. But he'd changed his mind. It had occurred to him André might be an ex-boyfriend, whom Nathalie had ditched. If André was still sore, that might explain their row after the rugby match.

The peace gesture had worked, so Steve now grabbed a plastic chair from a nearby table and watched André and Le Prof exploring mazes and fighting monsters. He cheered when André blew up another monster. They had been playing games for several minutes when Steve looked up to see Nathalie threading her way towards them between tables.

She winked at him. "D'you want a chat? I've got something to tell you."

Steve looked at André, to judge his reaction to this invitation. André glanced up, gave an almost dismissive toss of his head and resumed playing the game. Keen to take this opportunity of Nathalie's company, Steve rose and followed her to a nearby table, which a group of students had just vacated.

Nathalie moved a mass of paper and cans from the table, sat in one of the plastic chairs and twirled her hair round her fingers. "You know, when your Maman started working in Le Pont I thought she wouldn't last more than a week. But she has."

Steve nodded. "She's trying to earn some money. My Papa does sod all."

"Washing up. It's a shitty job. But I thought she and Papa were getting friendly." Nathalie laughed.

There was something about the laugh that made Steve uneasy. "What d'you mean?"

" I reckon they're fucking."

"What!"

Nathalie nodded. "I was going to bed last night and I heard them in Papa's room. Talking and laughing."

Steve sensed the blood rising to his face and grasped the edge of the plastic table to steady himself. Surely his mother wouldn't

151

have sex with another man. He'd always thought he could rely on her to be sensible and hard working, whatever Dad did. There must be some mistake. "Maman wouldn't do that. Anyway, isn't she too old?"

Nathalie laughed. "I think she's quite good-looking for her age. And I'm not surprised about Papa. He's been on his own since Maman left. I could tell he liked Alison by the way he looked at her. "

"Fuck them!" Steve brought his right fist down on the table with enough force to make it shake.

André looked up from his game, and other students turned to see what was happening.

"Hey, don't do that!" said Nathalie. "It's only sex, and maybe love. Is that so bad?"

"They've fucked me up, my parents. First, they dragged me to France..."

"What's wrong with France?"

Steve noticed the alarm in Nathalie's face and realised he didn't want to frighten her. "Sorry. It's just I didn't know anyone to start with. And Papa never got a proper job. Just sat at home, drinking. I thought Maman had more sense. But she hasn't. Not if she's fucking your Papa."

"Look, I didn't think you'd take it that way." Nathalie laid her slim hand on top of his. "I didn't realise your parents had made a mess of your life."

He looked into her dark eyes and knew he didn't want her feeling sorry for him. " Don't worry about me. I'll be all right." He put his left hand on top of hers.

She nodded. "I was cut up after Maman left. But I got over it. You realise parents are just people."

Behind them, André gave a yell. "We're up to the next level."

For a moment, Steve lifted his head and wished he was still playing computer games with André. That was much more straightforward than understanding people. Of course, he'd recognised his father's failings over the last two years, which was painful, because he was still fond of him. Was he going to have to reconsider his attitude to his mother as well? Had he expected too much of her? The question confused and grieved him, so he shelved it and concentrated on stroking Nathalie's hand.

"I like Alison,"she said. "I didn't mean to cause trouble for her."

"No. I don't want Maman hurt." Steve was clear about that. He still wanted to protect his mother if he could. Whatever happened.

"So don't say anything to her. And don't say anything to your Papa. Or you'll cause real trouble." Nathalie withdrew her hand from between his.

The bell for the afternoon lessons sounded.

"I won't, I promise," Steve said. "But can we stay friends?" He didn't want his angry outburst to upset her, or give the impression he was always bad tempered.

She smiled and stood up. "Course."

As Steve stomped towards the classroom for the next lesson, he scarcely noticed the other students, or the rain tracing down the windows of the corridor. He hadn't realised how much he'd come to rely on his mother, as his disillusion with Dad increased. The shock of her disloyalty was so much worse, because she'd been so reliable, prepared to listen to him and advise if needed. It felt like a betrayal. The idea of her having sex with a man other than her husband disgusted him.

He sat in the class, which was boring history, and wondered

why he was so offended. It wasn't that he was against sex in general. Nathalie seemed almost amused by what had happened. He remembered meeting her father when he'd gone mushrooming with the Ricauds. A tall, dark man who'd talked to him about mushrooms and wild boar. She'd made her father sound strict, but surely that didn't fit with fucking another man's wife? The idea occurred to Steve that, if Nathalie's father could have sex with his mother, there might be a chance for him with Nathalie. It was all right for young people to muck around, but he'd expected his mother to know better. Was it her age that was the problem, or was he perhaps jealous? Steve dismissed this idea with disgust.

Of course, his father was behaving stupidly and perhaps it was unfair to expect his mother to stick with him forever. But, if his mother had sex with Nathalie's father, didn't that risk bringing the whole shaky structure of their family down in ruins? He imagined Mum and Dad shouting and fighting. What would happen to him in those circumstances? Steve reminded himself he was sixteen, fit and bright enough to be coping in a French school. He would survive, despite the stupidity of his parents.

*

Steve had been looking forward to riding his new scooter but it didn't stop him getting wet on his way home from school. By the time he arrived, his yellow jacket was streaming with water and his jeans were soaked. There was no sign of Dad, apart from a bottle of wine on the kitchen table. Steve realised he'd have to shower, change, then prepare something to eat for two. Dad's failure to get dinner only cranked Steve's anger further. He wandered round the room, picking up plates and mugs, feeling he wanted to break something. Anything.

It had been difficult to contain his anger at school and the wet ride home hadn't improved his mood, as every car that passed had drenched him with muddy water. Not that he was going to complain with Mum around. It had proved difficult to persuade her to buy a scooter with Gran's money and he didn't want to admit some of her reservations were right. She'd thought it would be expensive to run and unsafe to ride. He'd promised to be careful. The thought reminded him why he was so angry with Mum. Her normal good sense had deserted her. Stopping at the table, he picked up the wine bottle and took a swig. That was what Dad did to forget the things that troubled him.

Apart from making him light headed, it made no difference. He swallowed another gulp, and was about to take a third when he remembered how angry it made him to see Dad drunk and incapable. Drink wasn't the solution. It was part of the problem. So he dashed the bottle to the ground and had the satisfaction of seeing it break in pieces on the quarry tiles.

A few moments later the door opened and Dad stood, gazing at the mess of glass and wine on the floor.

"What the hell's going on?"

"I'm sick of the lot of you," grumbled Steve.

"What have I done to deserve this?" Dad gestured at the broken glass.

In a moment Steve's anger turned to confusion, as he realised he couldn't explain. However stupidly Mum had behaved he couldn't betray her secret, as the consequences were hard to contemplate.

"Sorry, Dad," Steve mumbled. "Things were going wrong at school. I'll clear the mess up." He took a rubbish bin from its place at the end of a kitchen unit and stooped to start clearing up the glass. As he stood up with a piece of broken glass in his hand, he saw fear in Dad's eyes. For a moment, Steve hesitated, aware the power in the house lay with him and wondered what would happen if he used it. The prospect filled him with horror and he dropped the glass into the bin.

Chapter 19

Brian walked out of the drive and stood at the corner, where the road began its descent into the valley. He didn't know what kind of car to watch for, as Tim and Helen were hiring at Toulouse Airport. Feeling ill at ease, he continued down the road, until the first bend at the edge of a plum orchard. He couldn't stop his guests seeing the barn, but wouldn't they come to the conclusion the *chambre d'hôte* project had failed? Could he persuade them otherwise? Though he'd thought of changing the plans and trying to bribe the Mayor, nothing had come of these ideas. Of course, it wasn't his fault. Jean-Claude Bouyssou was a cheat and the Mayor a bloody-minded bureaucrat. But how to convince Tim and Helen? As he walked back up the hill, he struggled to think of a positive gloss to put on the situation. It wasn't easy. Although he'd promised Alison not to drink before lunch, he yearned to find a bottle of something.

The weather was discouraging, with rain clouds drifting in from the west, making the white limestone walls look grey and the garden bedraggled with fallen leaves. When he went inside, Alison complained about his muddy footprints on the newly cleaned floor. He sensed she shared his nervousness about her brother's arrival, as she spent the morning cleaning: scrubbing quarry tiles, vacuuming and cleaning windows. Her activity only contributed to his anxiety.

It was mid afternoon when a black Renault Megane came up the hill, turned the corner and stopped on the drive. Brian hurried to greet his guests. Helen emerged first, neat in navy trousers with matching jacket and shoes. A moment later, Tim unfolded himself from the driving seat, then opened the boot to take out two cases. Although looking relaxed, in a sweatshirt and chinos, his limp was noticeable.

"Welcome to St Thomas," Brian said, throwing his arms out wide, in an effort to give the impression of an affable host. He shook hands with Tim and gave Helen an awkward peck on the cheek, catching a hint of some floral perfume.

Alison hurried out of the kitchen and embraced her brother and sister-in-law. "Did you have a good journey?"

"We got a bit lost in Toulouse Airport," said Tim. "After that, it was easy."

Alison smiled. "We get lost there too. It changes all the time."

To delay awkward questions about the barn, Brian made himself busy, picking up Tim and Helen's cases and leading the way into the house.

As Helen stepped into the kitchen, she looked at the beamed ceiling, the wood-fronted units and the big table." This is lovely."

"The table's big enough to seat ten, "said Brian. Although Helen's manner was pleasant, he wondered if she was calculating what everything had cost. True, it had been expensive but it was an investment. Or had been.

On the way through the living room he pointed out the natural stone walls and copper-covered chimney breast. Dumping the cases in the biggest bedroom, Brian gestured at the double bed, with its terracotta-coloured duvet, and the real oak wardrobe, which had cost them far more than they could afford. "Make yourself at home. But there's tea and apple flan in the kitchen if you like."

158

Having returned to the kitchen, Brian stood by the table, fiddling with the packet of Marlboros in his pocket and getting in the way of Alison, who was cutting slices of flan. Soon, everyone was seated at the table, drinking English tea. Brian tried to encourage conversation about the weather and the health of both families.

"I'm trying to persuade Mum to move nearer to us,"said Tim and gave a rueful smile. "But she's stubborn."

Alison nodded. "She likes her independence. But she doesn't want us to neglect her. It's difficult."

"She's still emerging from the shadow of your father," said Helen.

"Yes, Dad had very decided ideas." Alison poured more tea.

The conversation had started to flag by the time Helen said: "Aren't you going to show us your grand renovation project?"

Brian glanced at Alison, aware the moment he'd dreaded couldn't be delayed longer.

"Of course," she said, stood up with a kind of defiance and led the way across the drive to the barn.

Brian opened the wooden doors with a creak and they walked in, stood in a group and stared. The place was a shell. The outer walls were grey and decrepit, the floor bare concrete, and bags of unused cement, piles of bricks and roof tiles lay stacked in one corner. Tim and Helen looked in the storage area, which was full of bicycles and shelves laden with tools, and then peered up to the roof, where massive oak beams met in a series of complex joints. On one of the beams, a black redstart's empty nest trailed pieces of grass. In corners, cobwebs hung in swathes, black with dust and loaded with leaves and dead insects.

Tim walked over to a wall and prodded the decaying mortar."You've got a way to go yet."

Brian indicated the roof with a wave of his hand. "We've had the roof retiled, and masses of concrete added to the foundations. We're just about to have the windows fitted."

"We were," said Alison, in a flat tone.

Tim turned towards her. "Did something go wrong? From what Brian said on the phone, I thought you were making progress."

"We're having to wait for the necessary permissions," said Brian, with an attempt at breeziness. "French bureaucracy takes for ever."

"No," said Alison. "The Mayor said no. He said we couldn't put windows in the front because it would spoil the surroundings of the church."

"I'm sure we can sort it out, " Brian said and glared at her, shocked by this betrayal. She'd never contradicted him in public like this before and her desertion left him floundering.

"So is your renovation project going ahead or isn't it?" Helen asked, the sharpness of her tone irritating.

He wasn't going to let her bully him. "I asked the architect to do some more work on the plans. And wrote to the Mayor. I've explained the project would bring people into the village."

Alison stood looking at the floor in silence, shaking her head as if unable to stop. In an attempt to comfort and stop her contradicting him, Brian tried to put his arm round her. She drew away and moved closer to her brother.

"Isn't the *chambre d'hôte* happening?" Tim asked.

"No," said Alison.

"So how are you living?"

Alison fumbled with her handkerchief. "Well, I'm earning

something from my job in the restaurant."

"You always were a good cook," said Helen.

"I'm washing up and doing simple preparation."

"Washing up?" asked Helen, raising a plucked eyebrow. "Couldn't you get anything better than that?"

"My French wasn't good enough. Written French anyway."

Alison and her relatives stood in a knot, discussing the problem Brian had wanted to avoid, leaving him isolated. Nothing like this had happened to him before, as he was used to his opinion mattering more than his wife's. He felt the vein in his neck beginning to throb.

"And what are you doing?" asked Helen turning towards him, her voice rising and a red spot glowing in her cheeks.

He drew himself up, trying to hold his own yet keep self-control. " I've looked at several ways to earn money. The best seems to be setting up a business selling antiques."

"Antiques?" asked Tim, with obvious incredulity. "I'm not sure how realistic that is."

"Well, I've only made one or two purchases so far. But I'm sure there's money to be made if you're careful." Brian was aware he was gabbling but couldn't stop himself. " It takes a certain amount of research and determination, of course."

"You'll need more than that to make a business."

"Give me time. It'll work out in the end. Trust me," said Brian. It was no use. He was losing the argument and felt the atmosphere in the barn growing tense and adversarial.

"Don't worry, Ali," said Tim, giving his sister's shoulders a squeeze. "We'll help. We'll look at ways you can sort this out. But I'll need to know what your financial position is."

"We can cope," said Brian, clenching his fists. He didn't want his in-laws taking over his life.

"You'll need advice," said Tim, his usual good-natured manner becoming stern. "You've borrowed money from us. And probably from other sources. How are you going to pay it back?"

"Of course we'll honour our debts." In fact, Brian had lost track of how much money they owed. It was Alison who'd pored over the papers and listed everything. He could feel himself giving way to panic.

The barn door opened and Steve walked in, pushing his scooter, his yellow jacket and blue jeans spattered with mud. He took off his helmet. "Hello. What are you all doing in here?"

"You're a bit grubby," said Helen but she walked over and gave him a kiss on the cheek. The tension in the barn began to ease a little.

"It's raining," said Steve.

Tim removed his arm from Alison's shoulders. "We'll have a chat later."

For a moment, everyone watched as Steve parked his scooter in the storage area, then returned with him to the house. Brian shut the door to the barn and stood in the drizzle. He'd never felt more lost in his adult life. It was as though the ground was giving way under his feet, leaving him falling through space alone and with no idea where he might land.

*

Dinner was awkward, although Alison hurried between table and cooker, serving the best food she could while trying to keep the tone civil. Brian drank too much and lectured Tim about the failings of President Nicolas Sarkozy, while Helen tried to persuade Steve to talk about school. Alison was aware of Tim watching her with a slight frown. Rather than share a bedroom with Brian and risk a major row, she resorted to carrying a sleeping bag and bedroll up to the writer's room.

The next morning, she was surprised when Tim and Helen joined her and Steve for breakfast, saying they'd like to go for a walk. Alison suspected they wanted to talk to her alone, as they said they didn't mind if Brian wasn't up and Steve was going to the Ricaud's. She warned Tim and Helen the morning air would be chill, and the paths would be muddy after rain. To her relief, when Helen joined her in the kitchen, she was wearing an anorak and boots, rather than her usual court shoes. Tim had brought a walking pole, which clattered on the road as they set out.

As they climbed the path up the hill, slanting light splashed colour on ash-white limestone banks. Most flowers were finished but juniper bushes still showed green and an occasional wall brown butterfly flitted in shafts of sunshine. Mist lingered in the valley below, leaving trees drifting like boats on a lake. Above, the château stood clear on its rock, and a flock of jackdaws flew from surrounding trees, cawing as they circled.

Helen stopped. "It's beautiful."

"I can believe you love this place," said Tim.

Alison nodded. "You should see the sunsets. Our garden faces west and you can sit and watch the sun go down."

Helen drew close to Alison. "But it's not really working out for you, is it?"

Alison hesitated. It would be a relief to tell the truth. She had faith in Tim's competence and would be glad of his advice. "Everything's falling apart."

"Do you know how much money you actually owe?" asked Tim.

" Brian stopped paying the mortgage. I've been trying to pay it but there are still gaps. As for the other debts..." She fizzled out, thinking of the savings she'd tried to make and the arguments she'd had with the bank.

Tim frowned. "You could lose your house if you owe money on the mortgage."

"Brian doesn't think that'll happen. Because we borrowed the money in England, he says they won't bother to try to repossess a house in France."

"I wouldn't rely on it," said Tim. "You can pursue debts abroad. My company has to chase them sometimes."

Alison thought about this as they walked through the wood at the top of the hill. Leaves were falling in flurries and lodging between tree roots, almost concealing the emerging red mushrooms. They stopped at the edge of the field which gave a view over the next valley, with its pattern of farms and orchards. Wood smoke rose from bonfires and mingled with wisps of mist rising from ponds. A tractor moved between the lines of trees in an orchard.

"I don't know how to convince Brian, " said Alison, at last.

"Do you still trust his judgement?" Helen asked, sharpness in her voice.

Alison was reluctant to discuss the state of her marriage. "So what do I do?" she asked, her voice emerging as a wail.

"Do you have equity in the house?" Tim asked.

Alison nodded. "We put in money from the sale of Brian's Dad's house."

"I'm afraid the best thing you can do is sell the house. It would be a good idea to sell it now, rather than wait for it to be repossessed. Do you get to hear the financial news here?"

A jay took off with an alarm call and flew across the field. Alison watched it disappear into trees lower down the slope. "I don't really listen to it."

Tim shook his head. "I've got my laptop here but I can't get a network. If I could, I'd show you some predictions. It looks as if there's a crash coming. The American mortgage market is in trouble and there's been a run on Northern Rock."

It occurred to Alison that Tim's business might not be as secure as she'd believed and he might need the ten thousand pounds she'd borrowed from him. "Oh dear, I don't know how I'm going to repay your loan."

"I can wait. It's the mortgage and your electricity bills you need to worry about. And Council Tax, or whatever the French equivalent is."

As Alison looked across the valley, a distant village on a hilltop emerged from the mist, lit by sudden sunshine. She hated the idea of leaving this place. "Is there anything else we can do? Other than sell the house?"

Tim shook his head. "I'm sorry Ali. But if you've got a lot of debts and not much income, you haven't got many options."

Helen took her arm. "Shall we walk on? It's getting a bit cold, standing here."

Alison was relieved the questions were over. Although most of the decisions had been Brian's she couldn't avoid blame. There were so many questions she should have asked, so many decisions she should have challenged. She'd supported him too uncritically.

From the edge of the field, they walked downhill through woods. As the mist dispersed, the colours grew brighter. Holly berries and rose hips shone red, while mosses edged the path in emerald and deep green.

"I'd be sorry to leave here," said Alison.

"Is there anywhere you could go?" asked Helen. "Could you stay with friends?"

Although Alison immediately thought of François, she dismissed the idea. She might be able stay at Le Pont, but what would happen to Steve? Besides, that would mean leaving Brian. If she suggested such an idea to him, what would be his reaction? His moods were growing ever more volatile.

"If you came back to England," said Tim, "we might be able to help."

Alison stopped walking and turned aside, hiding her anxiety by examining mushrooms growing by a tree root. She was sure leaving France would mean breaking up her family. Brian wouldn't want to sell the house, let alone return to England and what would happen to Steve's education? " I don't know," she said at last. " I'll think about it. I'll have to talk to Brian."

"Do you want us to talk to him?" asked Helen.

Alison shook her head. "It would be better if I did."

"I'm sorry to be such uncomfortable guests." said Helen. "But we felt we had to say something. After what happened in the barn yesterday."

Alison sighed. "I know we're in trouble. I just didn't know what to do about it."

"We'll help in any way we can," said Tim.

They reached a place where the path forked, one branch leading down to a nearby village, and the other following the ridge.

"Do you want to go on?" Alison asked. "You can follow this path for miles."

"We've probably gone far enough," said Tim.

Alison nodded and turned to climb back up the slope. She spent the rest of the walk in silence, disentangling the threads of this crisis. Was there any way forward that wasn't fraught with difficulty? One thing was clear in her mind: she didn't want to let Steve down. She'd tried to give him a secure childhood and, although her influence over him was already waning, she'd do what she could to ensure he had a decent future. If she was honest with herself, she'd abandoned hope of Brian taking sensible decisions. Maybe their future did lie in separation. That suggested turning to François, but did he offer a solution to her problems? Although she cared for him, she couldn't move in with him and leave Steve stranded. However much she thought, her next step remained the same. She needed to talk to Brian.

Chapter 20

At eleven o'clock on Monday morning, Brian parked outside the antique shop on the road to Castelnau and opened the door to the converted barn. He carried his glass trinket dish, wrapped in tissue paper. He'd looked in the *Pages Jaunes* for shops selling antiques and second-hand goods but reluctantly decided to start with this place. Although the woman had looked at him with contempt, she'd bought the clock. He made sure he looked presentable, brushing his hair, cleaning his glasses and changing into a check shirt and grey trousers.

As he drove, he'd rehearsed his grievances against Tim and Helen. He resented their interference in his affairs. Helen was worse than her husband. She might have studied psychology and worked as a personnel manager, but that didn't give her the right to treat him like an errant employee. He was even angrier with Alison for her betrayal, contradicting him in public. That was outrageous. After such a setback, it was essential for him to restore his credibility in the eyes of his family. Although they might dismiss his ideas for making money, he was going to prove them wrong, by getting the best possible price for the trinket dish.

When he stepped into the barn, he found the display had changed. Some of the smaller objects were grouped on a big table, as a collection of gifts. He remembered the teddy bear, but it was surrounded by a doll's house, several vases in cut glass and china, and a clock. Brian walked over to look at the clock, thinking there was something familiar about it. He examined the brass case, hinged carrying handle, Roman numerals. There was no mistake. It was the clock he'd brought here, but priced at one hundred and fifty Euros.

He was still staring at the clock when the office door opened and the woman walked out, immaculate in a black dress teamed with a red and black patterned shawl. Brian watched her advancing with loathing. She'd cheated him: looked at him, decided he was an ignoramus, and given him less than the clock was worth. He wasn't going to settle for that treatment again, so he waited until she came close, then turned on his heel and walked out with his head held high.

After sitting in the car with a Marlboro to calm himself, Brian drove back to Caillac and stopped in the car park near the river. As he climbed the steps to the road, he glanced at the parade of shops which included Le Pont. The thought of Alison washing up there made him even angrier, as he should be able to make more money than she did. He strode along the main street, looking for the second antique shop on his list. At first, he missed the side street. The shop was squeezed between a laundrette and a boarded up restaurant.

A glance convinced him this shop was a very different place, unlikely to be snobbish. The paint round the window frame might have been white once, but it was so chipped and dirty the effect was grey-brown. The window was crammed with a mixture of items: a stack of old tables, a chair with a carved back and a fire back featuring a flame breathing dragon.

As Brian entered, an old man sat at a desk, studying a watch with an eye glass. A lamp beside him cast a light which showed every vein and wrinkle on his face, as well as thousands of tiny dust specks that drifted through the beam. Brian made his way between cases full of glass and china and a stack of agricultural implements he didn't recognise. The old man looked at him with watery eyes but didn't speak. Brian unwrapped his trinket dish and laid it on the desk, where the light made the opalescent glass

169

shine and showed every detail of the plumage of the owl in the centre.

"I'm interested in selling this."

The old man turned it over and examined it with his eye glass. "I'll give you twenty Euros ."

"Only twenty? it's Lalique."

"Twenty Euros."

Having stood undecided for a minute, Brian picked up the trinket dish. "I'll leave it for now," he said and left.

If he sold the ornament for twenty Euros, he'd only made five. That wasn't enough. It looked as if he'd meet this obstacle at every step: the need to deal with middle men. Even if they weren't all crooks, he should have realised they would cream off a good profit. Maybe he needed to try a different approach, taking a stall at a *brocante* sale and selling direct to the public. That would need investment. He'd have to buy a number of items, perhaps specializing in something like clocks, and he'd need a van, a small one to start with.

At that thought, he grew disconsolate. It would be difficult to persuade Alison of the sense of buying a selection of antiques, but a van would be out of the question. Although she'd bought Steve a scooter, her mother had provided the cash and was hardly going to extend the same generosity to him. He'd set aside a little money to put down as a deposit for his own vehicle, since he decided cycling wasn't an option but still didn't have enough. Brian stopped at the Café de la Place for a Pastis and a chance to consider his next move.

*

Alison had kissed Tim and Helen goodbye with reluctance.

During their visit, they'd provided her with support and protection against Brian. She was beginning to think she needed it, as Brian's resentment crackled. By the time they drove away, Steve had gone to school but Brian stood by the kitchen door, waving. She was relieved when he decided to go to Caillac to sell his trinket dish, as it suited her to be in the house alone, catching up with household tasks before she went back to work. She'd scrounged Saturday off work, which made her feel she was letting François down, as it was the busiest day at Le Pont. It would be good to be back.

She heard a vehicle drawing up outside, looked out of the kitchen door and waved to the young woman in the yellow *Poste* van. Having collected the post, she lay it on the kitchen table and sorted it into piles. Apart from brightly coloured flyers from local shops, there were several bills and a letter from the bank. As soon as she opened it, the words "We will seek possession" glared out at her. She slumped into a chair and plunged her head into her hands.

On a second reading, she realised she could still negotiate with the bank, offer to pay a little more each month. That wouldn't help much. She felt she was pouring money into a hole that was always growing. Brian's attempts to sell antiques offered just a few Euros profit on a clock or a trinket dish, and would never fill that hole. They were running out of options. It looked as if Tim had been right in saying they needed to sell the house. But how to convince Brian? The more she considered that question, the more her mind filled with foreboding.

She made leek and potato soup for lunch, because it was cheap and ate her portion when Brian was late. His lateness angered her. She imagined him in a bar somewhere, filling himself up with drink. After a while, she took the letter from the bank upstairs to the writer's room and added it to the pile of financial papers on the desk. She was sitting at the computer looking at the spreadsheet she'd compiled when she heard the kitchen door bang. Collecting the whole pile of papers, she hurried downstairs.

Brian stood near the cooker, smelling of alcohol.

"You've been drinking again," she said, dumping the papers on the kitchen table.

"Not much. Only a glass."

"More than that, by the smell of it."

"I got here didn't I?" His tone was belligerent.

Alison handed him the latest letter, in an attempt to raise the question of the debts before the conversation grew angry . "I got this letter from the bank. It says they're going to repossess the house."

He glanced at it and threw it on the kitchen table. " It's a trick. They're only trying to frighten us. That's what they do. "

Guessing he hadn't even read it, she pressed on. "That's not what Tim said."

Brian's face flushed. "Oh, so that's why you went for a walk with Tim and Helen, is it? I wondered why I wasn't included. It looked as if they thought I wasn't good enough for them."

"They're my relatives rather than yours."

"Helen's a bitch."

"No she's not. She can be a bit sharp, that's all." Alison laid her hands on the papers, emphasising their importance. The discussion was getting out of control, veering away from the point she needed to make. "Look Brian, don't let's argue about this. It's too important."

"I won't listen to your brother and his bitchy wife telling us how to run our lives. They can get lost."

"Tim and Helen were saying we need to sell the house," she said, determined not to give in.

He pounded the table with his fist. "No, no, no."

"Otherwise it's going to be repossessed. Tim said they could repossess a house in France."

"Tim said." The vein in Brian's neck throbbed. "Why should your precious brother know more than me?"

"He's running a business. A successful business. He knows a lot about financial things. And he said there's a crash coming."

Brian took a step towards her, caught her by the arm and marched her out of the kitchen door and into the back garden. Standing beside her, he gestured at the orchard and the valley beyond. "Do you want to lose all this? After all the work we've put in? I don't think so."

Uncertain sunlight picked out the red tinge of Virginia Creeper in hedges and the pink tiles on the roofs of houses beyond the orchard. On the far side of the valley, plum trees marched in lines, their branches bare of leaves, towards the ragged woods that crowned the ridge.

"No. But we mightn't have any choice. Tim thought it would be better to sell now rather than be forced to sell later."

"I'm not going to sell up. How many times do I have to say that? Not now. Not ever."

"Than what the hell are we supposed to do?"

"We work our bloody socks off."

The comment angered Alison further. She couldn't work any harder. "You mean I do. It's me that does all the work if you haven't noticed. Have you even managed to sell that trinket dish?"

"You're getting as bitchy as your damned sister-in-law. It's as much your fault as mine, you know." He pulled her round to face him. "Wasn't the *chambre d'hôte* your idea in the first place?"

"Don't Brian. That hurt!" Alison wrenched her arm free and hurried away into the orchard.

She was shocked he'd hurt her. He'd never done so before but his moods were growing darker. Of course he'd suffered a series of disappointments, but the drink made things worse. As for his comment that the *chambre d'hôte* was her idea, was that true? She no longer remembered. The dream of coming to France was his but they'd discussed many ways to realise it. Some had been his ideas, some hers. It didn't matter at the time, because it had been a shared enterprise. Now it was tearing them apart.

She came to a stop under one of the old trees, her trousers wet from the damp grass. Leaves were falling and joining rotten fruit in sodden masses underfoot. Winter was coming, imposing its stark lines and muted colours on the landscape. Although it would be cold in the house, she could light a fire in the grate and cook warming food, but she dreaded the possibility of being evicted in the middle of winter. She had a vision of sitting on a box of possessions in pouring rain, while men carried furniture out. If she was going to have to leave, she wanted to go in her own time. As she looked back at the house, standing square at the top of the slope, she wondered whether the place she loved was entangling them, like some creeping plant.

Chapter 21

When Brian offered to go shopping, Alison looked at him with pursed lips, then insisted he didn't spend their money on wine. In fact, he had a different motive. He'd been left shocked by her readiness to sell the house. The idea of selling hadn't occurred to him and he would fight to keep it. But it would be good to talk to someone else and Carrie might be sympathetic. He wasn't sure what to say to her, but thought he could make the idea of selling look like some sick joke. If only it was. So he decided to call into the English library at Beaumont, after shopping, to return the antiques book and see Carrie.

At the library, the blue blinds had been rolled up and the room looked somehow smaller in the plain light of day. Its white walls and parallel lines of shelves were drab and some of the books worn. An elderly woman with short, grey hair and a plum-coloured jersey was sitting at the desk. She looked at him over her half-moon glasses and said Carrie was no longer working there. Too late, he remembered Carrie saying she wanted to spend more time painting.

Frustrated, Brian crossed the square and walked up the cobbled street. Most of the bright summer flowers had gone, leaching the colour out of the street scene and emphasising peeling paintwork on doors and shutters. He knocked on the door of Carrie's studio and waited. A minute or so elapsed before Carrie appeared, wearing her painting clothes: stained jeans, a loose navy jersey and a blue and white scarf over her hair.

As she looked at him, the corners of her mouth drooped. "Sorry, Brian, I really can't talk to you now."

"Are you in so much hurry? Are you painting the Mona Lisa or something? "he asked, with an attempt at lightness.

"I'm getting some paintings ready for an exhibition on Saturday. Can't you come back next week?"

"It would be nice to chat, but I can come back." Brian lingered in the doorway for a few moments. "Good luck with your exhibition."

At last she smiled but some of her former warmth had gone. "You can always phone."

As he trudged back down the hill, his sense of desolation increased. There was no one he could turn to now both the women in his life had deserted him. All he could do was adjourn to the Café des Voyageurs for a Pastis or two. It wasn't a pretentious place. The white walls bore a shimmer of yellow grease and the plastic covers of the chairs were ripped in places, but that was part of its attraction. Nobody bothered him as he sat at a table with a chipped plastic surface and drank as much as he liked. A skinny girl leant on the bar, playing with her hair as she waited for orders and a group of men lingered over drinks. One Pastis followed the first but they did no more than blur the edges of his frustration.

When he strolled back to the car, Brian wasn't worried about driving home. It wasn't the first time he'd driven home after a few drinks and he knew the road. He took the bends carefully on the road over the ridge and reckoned his driving was still good. As he climbed the next ridge and approached a roundabout in the village of Bournac, he noticed two gendarmes. They were standing, distinctive in their navy uniforms, next to a van on the gravel outside the Gendarmerie. Of course, they had every right to be there but the village was so quiet, it was unusual to see any activity. Perhaps they were looking for speeding motorists, while he was keeping below the limit.

A gendarme took a step into the road and raised his hand.

"Shit." Brian slowed to a stop, hoping that if he behaved courteously, they wouldn't know he'd been drinking. He opened the car window.

The gendarme handed him a breathalyser. "Breathe into this please, Monsieur."

Brian felt his hands trembling as he took a deep breath and blew.

The gendarme looked at the changing colour of the breathalyser. "Get out of the car."

It was no use arguing with the gendarme, who stood at the car door with a grim face and a revolver at his side. As Brian stepped out of the car, he almost stumbled.

"You are double the legal limit," said the gendarme, holding up the breathalyser. "You can't drive in this condition."

"That can't be right, Monsieur. I didn't drink more than one glass and I was driving sensibly," said Brian, trying to sound convincing.

Ignoring his protest, the gendarme produced an official form and filled it in. "You'll get a fine and a driving ban."

Brian stared at the road through the village and thought how marooned he felt when Alison had the car. "A driving ban? I can't live round here without driving. We're miles away from anywhere."

The gendarme shrugged and returned to the van. Brian watched as a couple of gendarmes pushed his car onto the gravel. He felt lost. Both his options appalled him: walking the seven kilometres back to St Thomas, or ringing Alison and see if she could meet him. He imagined her working in the garden or preparing lunch and knew she'd be furious. But she would need to retrieve the car. In the end, Brian reached into the car and fumbled in the glove box. Among the maps and garage till receipts was a small bottle of Armagnac, which he put in his pocket. At last, he found his phone. He took off his glasses, wiped them with his handkerchief and put them back on.

"I'm afraid I've got a bit of a problem," he said as Alison answered.

"What's happened?" He heard the alarm in her voice.

"Well, I was driving home, quite sensibly, when I got pulled over by the gendarmes."

"Don't tell me you'd been drinking."

"I was just unlucky. Could happen to anybody." Brian was aware of the pleading tone in his voice but couldn't change it.

"You idiot. I've told you not to drink if you're driving."

He paused. " I'm afraid they gave me a fine and a driving ban. Don't worry, I'll find the money to pay the fine."

"I don't know where from. Where are you anyway?"

"Bournac."

"What on earth are you doing there?"

"I went shopping, then I took the antiques book back to the library in Beaumont. That's all." Brian wiped his face with his handkerchief.

"And saw Carrie, I suppose."

"She wasn't there. She doesn't work there any longer."

"But they won't let you drive home, will they?"

"I'm a bit stuck. Can't you come here and pick up the car?"

There was a pause. "I've a mind to leave you to walk home. But I need the car. So I'll have to pick you up, if I can beg Albert for a lift. It'll be a while."

Brian stood shivering, buffeted by cold winds which chased across the forecourt of the Gendarmerie. It formed the centre of a row of three old limestone buildings. On one side was the Mairie, flying the traditional tricoleur, while a restaurant occupied the other. For a while he looked through the window of the restaurant, at the bar with its bottles and glasses and the rows of metal tables. It was no use. He couldn't let Alison find him in a bar after what had happened. The next exit from the roundabout led past a hairdressers, a general store and houses with closed shutters. Although the wind rattled the sign outside the shop and drove a few drops of sleety rain into his face, he decided to walk some distance along the road and back . Where the houses ended in fields and a graveyard, he stopped and took a swig of Armagnac from the bottle of his pocket. Alison wouldn't know about that.

It didn't improve his mood. He realised a fine and driving ban would give him a disadvantage in his arguments with Alison. She would use them as evidence in favour of selling the house. That would be a devastating loss. The house wasn't just a status symbol. Brian remembered the glee with which his father had bought their council house in 1980. For Eddie, buying a home of his own meant he'd climbed up the social ladder.

The house in St Thomas, on the other hand, epitomised Brian's dream of a life in France. Before they'd left England, he'd imagined sitting under a tree with a glass of wine, doing a little writing and looking out over a landscape of vineyards or fields and woods. The *chambre d'hôte* would make enough money to cover the bills and, although there'd be a bit of maintenance, it wouldn't be too onerous. When he saw the old house in St Thomas, he thought he'd found a place that matched his dreams.

It hadn't turned out that way but selling the house meant the end of his dreams. Finished.

***

After Brian's telephone call, Alison sat at the desk in the living room and thought about the conversation she'd had with François on Saturday. For the first time, they'd sneaked up to the flat together after the lunchtime shift ended and the other cooks and waiters had dispersed. The shutters had been open, giving a view of the river and an old warehouse on the south bank. In daylight the flat was scruffier than she'd realised. The fabric of the sofa was marked by unravelling threads and there was a layer of dust on shelves. She didn't mind because she felt warm and safe with François. There was nothing false or pretentious about him, so she could trust him. She had drawn the duvet over both of them and given an account of Tim and Helen's visit, from their tour of the barns to Tim's advice that she sell the house.

He propped himself up one elbow. "If I thought only of myself I would say leave Brian and come and live with me. But it would be difficult, wouldn't it? You need to think of your son. And I need to think of my family and everyone here."

 Alison stroked the hair on his chest. " I like being with you. But I couldn't stay here."   There was nowhere for Steve at Le Pont.

"But if you leave Brian, you're saying to everyone your marriage is over. He'll have to sell the house."

These words returned to Alison, as she crossed the road to the Couzineau's. Although leaving Brian was a last resort, she felt she was reaching that place. He was sliding into alcoholism, and the more drunk he became the more erratic his behaviour. Not only was it difficult to deal with him without losing her temper, but she'd begun to worry about her safety and Steve's.

It took Alison a while to find Albert Couzineau. Neither he nor Valérie were at home and it was only when Alison heard voices from the open door of the church she realised they were there. As she entered, light from a stained glass window created a coloured pattern on the stone floor. A plaster statue of the Virgin was the only other ornament. Valérie was dusting the plain wooden chairs, while Albert swept the nave with a broom. Short and wiry, he could have passed for a much younger man, except for a wisp of white hair and wrinkled skin.

Alison made an apologetic plea for a lift, while he lent on his broom and listened, his clear blue eyes studying her face.

"It's a temptation, alcohol," he said, his voice neutral. But he left his broom, returned with her to his house and backed his car out of the garage.

Fifteen minutes later, Alison stepped out of Albert's old Renault in Bournac and saw Brian standing forlorn by their car. She regarded him, plump and red-faced, with his hands in his jacket pockets and could hardly control her anger.

"So what's your excuse?" she demanded.

"It's not going to happen again. I'll make sure it doesn't. " He looked down at the gravel.

"You'll be banned."

"Maybe the gendarmes won't notice if I drive a bit. They're not very vigilant, are they? Most of the time they just stand around."

Brian's ability to hang on to a thread of hope had been one of his endearing qualities but now it was infuriating. Alison opened the car door. "Get in."

She drove home in silence, her hands clenched on the steering wheel.

As soon as they reached the kitchen, she put her hands on her hips and faced him. "I'm fed up with this. All you're doing is drinking and spending money we haven't got."

"I'll have another shot at selling antiques. I've had a bit of success. It'll just take..."

She gave a contemptuous snort, aware his plans would fall through if he couldn't drive. "You're not going to get far like that. It's not going to meet our debts. We'll have to sell the house."

Brian clenched his hands and his face flushed. " No. You'll have to sell it over my dead body."

Alison picked up a bowl of lettuce standing on a work surface and held it out like an exhibit. "Look, I was getting lunch while you were drinking. I've been propping you up. It's time I called it a day. I need to look after myself and Steve. I'm leaving if you don't agree to sell the house."

He gazed at her, his mouth hanging open for several moments. "Leaving me? You can't be serious."

"Yes I am."

"Don't be bloody stupid. We've got into this mess together and we'll sort it out together."

"No we won't. I'm tired of waiting for you to do something sensible. I'm going." Alison put the bowl of salad back on the work surface but, as she grasped the handle of the living room door, Brian took a step towards her and seized her wrist.

"You can't leave me. You wouldn't cope without me." His face was red and she could smell the alcohol on his breath.

"Don't you believe it. It's you that's not coping." She pulled away and opened the door.

"Fucking bitch!" Brian picked up the bowl of salad and threw it, just missing her head as she stepped through the doorway, filling her ears with the sound of breaking glass and sprinkling her face with salad dressing.

Chapter 22

After dinner Steve shut himself in his room, on the excuse he had homework. That was true but his real reason was a need to escape from his parents. As soon as he'd arrived from school, he realised there was something wrong. Although his mother had prepared a chicken stew, there was an edgy atmosphere as they sat down in the kitchen to eat. His parents didn't look at each other and rarely spoke, while his mother's eyes were red as if she'd been crying. They'd obviously had some kind of row, which wasn't unusual, and he wondered about its cause. It wasn't his fault. At least, he hoped not. True, he was grumpy when he thought about François fucking his mother, which he did from time to time, but he'd been careful not to say anything to Dad. Nevertheless, the row was sure to affect him in some way. Best to keep his head down.

He took his school books out of his rucksack, dumped them on the small desk and sat on the rickety chair. For a while, he looked at the wildlife drawings and photos arranged on the walls, with a recent sketch of a buzzard at the centre of the display. He was proud of his pictures and wanted a chance to add more, but tonight he had nothing new to draw and he had physics homework. At least it wasn't history or French literature, which were the worst. Before he started work, he turned on his CD player: Iron Maiden. As Dad hated heavy metal and it wouldn't be a good idea to annoy him, Steve put his headphones on. The music wrapped him in waves of sound, isolating him from his parents and their problems.

As he read his homework assignment, his mother opened the

door and slipped in.

It was unusual for her to come in uninvited, though Dad did. Steve took his headphones off. "You might have knocked."

"I did." She stood close to his chair and pointed to the picture of the buzzard on the wall. "That's good."

"Thanks." He was uneasy, suspecting she had a reason for coming into his room.

She stood for a while, as if undecided, before speaking again. "Steve, there's something I want to say to you."

"I'm not in trouble or anything, am I?"

"No, you're doing fine. It's your Dad and I that are in trouble." She sat down on the edge of his bed, ignoring the duvet, which lay on the floor in a red and black striped heap. " You know we're always short of money?"

"Course."

"We owe a lot to banks and people. I don't know how we can ever pay it."

She looked strained, the sinews in her slim neck showing. In an attempt to help, he made the only offer he could."D'you want me to leave school and get a job after all?" Immediately, he realised he'd be sorry to leave now he'd made friends and was doing well.

"I think we need to sell the house, move somewhere else."

"Can we move to Caillac? I'd be nearer my friends." Steve had never understood his parents' enthusiasm for the house in St Thomas. True, it was bigger than their house in Bromley, with more space for bikes and sports gear, but it was too far from anywhere. Nothing happened.

His mother almost crumpled, plunging her head in her hands.

"I can't persuade your Dad we need to sell. He won't face it."

Steve sat in silence, surprised by her confession. Although he might think Dad was a lazy drunk, his mother didn't say so. Not in front of him. Either Mum had decided to treat him as an adult, or things were getting worse. When he thought of the fraught atmosphere he'd found on returning home, he suspected the latter.

"I've told your Dad I'm thinking of leaving him," she said slowly, as if considering every word. "If we're separated, Dad will have to sell the house."

Steve stared at her. " Leave Dad? What d'you mean? You're not coming back?" The memory of Nathalie's story burst into his mind. He stood up, knocking his chair over and towering over his mother, while a flood of angry words burst from his mouth before he could stop them. "Oh, I understand! You're going to live with that man, Nathalie's papa. He's been fucking you."

Her face flushed red. "Steve!"

"Did you think I didn't know? Nathalie told me."

"It's not like that."

"Isn't it? Sounds like it to me. I thought you had more sense than Dad. Then I found out about Nathalie's papa..." He stopped because her shoulders were trembling and she had covered her eyes with her hands. Immediately he regretted causing her pain.

His mother stood, her eyes red and wrapped her arm round his shoulders. "Look, whatever happens I want you to be all right."

Steve shook himself free of her embrace. "Are you going to live at that restaurant, with that man?" A moment later, it occurred to him Le Pont was Nathalie's home. They would be close.

"I'll find rooms somewhere. You can come with me. Or you can stay with your Dad. You ought to have a say. "

As Steve thought about living alone with Dad, he remembered times they'd rowed and nearly come to blows. His mind filled with visions of knives and blood on the floor. It wouldn't work. "I don't want to stay here with Dad. It's not that I hate him or anything. It's just that ..." On an impulse, he picked up his rucksack and started stuffing it with clothes and school books. "I might be better off out of here."

"Where are you going? You can't just leave," she said, her voice rising in alarm.

He dropped his rucksack, realising he had no plan in mind. "I dunno what I want to do. Sorry Mum."

*

A wet ride to school the next day didn't improve Steve's mood. As his scooter pottered down the long hill from St Thomas to Caillac the wind blew hard from the north west, carrying a cold rain which stung his face. Muddy water splashed his legs. It was little quicker on the scooter and he got colder without the exercise of cycling. He was beginning to think he should have let Mum book a place on the bus for the winter term. After the row they'd had, the thought she was sometimes right annoyed him. He was fed up with both his parents and wished he didn't have to return home to the arguments and tension. It felt as if some meltdown was coming. If so, he wouldn't know what to do. His instinct was to get out but part of him thought he ought to stay to look after Mum. He didn't know what Dad might do if he'd drunk too much. Life was getting very complicated.

By the time Steve reached the *lycée* he was spattered all over with mud. He locked his scooter and hurried to the main block, which looked as bleak as a tombstone in the rain. He darted along the corridor to the changing room, hoping Nathalie wouldn't see him. She took care to look good, even at school, with her hair in a pony tail and studs in her ears. He could imagine her laughing at his dishevelled state. As Steve opened his locker and pulled out clean trousers and shoes, André strolled in, carrying a helmet and wearing black waterproofs, splashed with mud.

André grinned. "You're wetter than me."

"Leave off." Although Steve was glad to be back on good terms with André, this morning he was aggrieved against the world.

"Your face looks like you've been rolling in shit." André opened his locker.

"Fuck off."

André started peeling off his waterproofs. "You're bad tempered today. What's got into you?"

Steve slammed the door of his locker. "It's my parents. They fight all the fucking time."

"My parents only argue about stupid things."

"Lucky."

André stepped out of his wet waterproofs and left them in a pool at his feet. "Come to my house."

"What about your parents?"

André shrugged. "They won't mind."

For Steve, the prospect of staying at the Ricaud's house was attractive. Not only could he play computer games with André, but also there weren't any rows at the Ricauds. He wasn't sure how they managed it, with André and his parents there, and various friends and relatives drifting in, but the contrast with his own house was striking. He took an immediate decision. "That'd be great."

*

By the time Steve arrived at the Ricaud's, the rain had fizzled out but light was fading, leaving the low-lying land near the Lot ghostly in mist. Even in the beam of his lights, the house and the wood behind it disappeared into twilight. Somewhere an owl hooted. He could see no-one but heard a tractor on the road. Perhaps Georges Ricaud was returning late from pruning his fruit trees, or planting new ones. Working, unlike his own Dad. Steve left his scooter propped next to a pile of neatly stacked logs under the overhanging roof of the barn. For a few moments he hesitated to knock on the front door, wondering if he'd really be welcome. He'd often spent whole days at the Ricaud's and sometimes stayed overnight, but he'd never turned up after school without warning.

André opened the door, wearing a clean sweatshirt and jeans. "Mum's in the kitchen. She wants to say hi."

"Is that bad?"

"Don't think so."

As Steve walked along a narrow hall to the kitchen, he was aware his shoes squelched. Murielle was sitting at the table, working at a laptop, with a pile of books beside her. With her glasses and her greying hair fastened in a pleat, she looked more like a teacher than a farmer's wife. André had said her real enthusiasm was local history.

She looked up and smiled at him. "You'd better go and have a shower."

Steve stood by the table, clenching and unclenching his hands. "Is it all right if I stay, Madame Ricaud?"

"You're welcome. But you ought to phone home, let your parents know where you are. They'll be worried about you."

"Yeah." Steve pictured Dad sitting in the writer's room reading and drinking, while his mother worked at Le Pont. Mum would be worried if she found him missing without explanation, while Dad would be angry.

Murielle nodded. " You can use our phone."

"Thanks."

For a while, Steve stood by the phone in the hall, which lay on a carved wooden cupboard. Nearby was a realistic china model of a red setter, which he stroked. He stared at family photographs on the walls, and the old-fashioned hall-stand with its rows of coats, jackets and umbrellas. It was difficult to know what to say to Dad. As there was no way he could repeat the conversation with his mother, his only course was to present his flight to the Ricaud's as a casual decision to go to a friend's house. But Dad had been in a bad mood since Tim and Helen's visit, so he might react angrily. Steve wasn't sure if he could cope with that.

"Hi, Dad," he said when Brian answered the phone. "I 'm just ringing to say I'm at the Ricaud's."

"Why the hell didn't you tell me before?"

The irritation in Dad's voice annoyed Steve. "What you fussing about ? I've just gone to a mate's house."

" I can't win with you, can I? When I go to the trouble of getting dinner, you can't be bothered to come home. But you make enough fuss if Mum's not here and I don't have dinner ready."

" Because you're always fucking drunk." Steve put the phone down.

190

Chapter 23

During the empty space of the afternoon, Brian brooded in the writer's room. In the morning, he'd managed to keep busy, working under the overhanging barn roof, chopping logs for winter. Since he'd realised wood fires were the best way of heating the living room, he'd taken to cutting and stacking firewood and was proud of his log pile. But hard physical work didn't stop him brooding. When the task was finished, he drifted up to the writer's room and sat at the desk with a glass of wine and a cigarette.

Alison's threat to leave spread poison through his mind. She'd proved such a source of support over the years, the prospect of her departure was like the diagnosis of serious illness. It threatened his whole way of life. The rational part of him wanted to persuade her to stay and drop her idea of selling the house. Yet he was so angry he could hardly speak to her civilly. She'd made such a fuss about the debts, although he'd assured her the creditors wouldn't try to enforce them. Threatening to leave was completely unreasonable. He hated her for it. He'd been the only breadwinner when Steve was little and had worked without complaint. Now she was the only person earning, she used that power to make demands on him. Sell the house or I'll leave. That was blackmail and he should resist.

On the desk lay his plan for selling antiques. It included the price of renting a stall in Caillac, together with dates and locations of sales of jumble and second hand goods in the area. All this was threatened by the driving ban. Brian took off his glasses and ran a hand through his thinning hair. After a few minutes, he tore up the plan and threw it in the waste paper basket. He needed to rethink. What else could he do?

In search of inspiration, he stood up and prowled round the writer's room, stopping to find his bottle of wine, stowed on a shelf. Nearby stood a photograph of his mother Marian, standing on Brighton Promenade, wearing a shirtwaister dress and a string of wooden beads, and laughing as her fair hair blew across her face. He'd idolised her. One of his earliest memories was sitting beside her on the sofa, as she sang nursery songs from a book, following the words with her finger. She'd left when he was twelve, without warning. He'd blamed his father, who had installed a step-mother, Val, who was always finding fault. At first, his mother kept in touch but her letters and phone calls had reduced to a trickle, then stopped.

When his father rang him at work, sixteen years after Marian left and said she'd died, Brian found he was mourning for someone whom he loved but no longer knew. Then he learned she'd spent periods in a mental hospital and felt part of his identity had been torn away. He had two ragged images of his mother which he couldn't piece together. Having thought Marian had left because of his father's infidelities, he was faced with the possibility her own instability was a factor. Worse, he'd traced his own creativity, his love of the arts and intellectual interests to his mother. If she had been unstable, what did that mean for him? He didn't want to follow this line of thinking. Instead, he put the photograph back in its place, sat at the desk and started compiling lists of jobs he could do.

As the sunset faded outside the dormer window, Brian got up to turn on the light. He realised it was time Steve came home, unless he'd spent another night at the Ricaud's without telling anybody. Brian padded down the stairs and headed for the light in the kitchen.

Steve was standing by the freezer, with a packet of lasagne in his hand. "I want something to eat. Are you going to have any?" he said.

"I thought you might be staying at the Ricaud's again."

"Nope."

"Did you just want to stay with a friend?" Brian watched Steve's face with suspicion. "Or was there some other reason?"

Steve stripped off the packaging and put the lasagne in the microwave, as if he hadn't heard the question.

"You might have told us. Instead of treating this place like a hotel." Brian couldn't keep the irritation from his voice.

"Leave off, Dad."

The evasiveness in Steve's manner increased Brian's unease. There was something he wasn't being told. Steve had been surlier than usual over the last few weeks and, although Alison had said it was just a phase, Brian didn't believe her. He suspected there'd been some communication between mother and son which had been kept from him. That niggled. He wanted to know what was going on. After a moment's thought, he decided the best way to persuade Steve to say more was to be patient but persistent. While the lasagne was cooking, Brian found some home grown leeks in the fridge, sliced and washed them and put them in a saucepan.

"Did something happen yesterday morning?" he asked, with an attempt at casualness.

Steve took plates, knives and forks out of the cupboard and put them on the kitchen table.

Brian's frustration grew. He knew his influence over his wife and son was draining away, leaving him powerless in his own house. In an attempt to stay calm, he drained the leeks and dished some out on the plates, while Steve took the lasagne out of the microwave. Having poured himself a glass of wine and sat down opposite his son, Brian watched Steve's chestnut hair fall over his eyes and wondered what he was hiding. He decided to attempt a light-hearted tone. "I wondered if you and Mum were plotting something."

"Nope." Steve ate a mouthful of lasagne, then raised his head. " I just like being at the Ricaud's."

"But you're our son. You belong here."

"Worse luck."

Despite Brian's attempts to stay calm, his voice rose. "I don't know what you're complaining of. We've looked after you, sent you to school..."

"Oh yeah? You brought me to France. That messed up my education. Then you ran out of money, so I can't have things like a laptop. Now you and Mum are falling out."

Brian swallowed a mouthful of wine and wondered if Alison had told Steve about her determination to sell the house. "Your mother's being unreasonable. Perhaps it's her age. Women can be like that."

" That's not what Mum said."

"What did your Mum say?"

Steve concentrated on his lasagne.

"I'm talking to you. You might try listening for once."

"Fuck off."

"Don't talk to me like that." Brian rose and glared at his son across the table.

Steve pushed back his chair and stood clenching and unclenching his fists, as if considering some violent action. After a few moments, he turned and strode towards the back door.

"I want to know what your mother said to you," said Brian, hurrying to the door to cut off Steve's escape route. "I think you're ganging up against me, the pair of you."

"She's fed up with you being so fucking useless and wants to leave." Steve's face reddened as he tried to push past his father.

"How dare you say that?" The vein in Brian's neck was throbbing.

Steve gave him a shove which made him reel and yanked the door open, heading into darkness.

"Where d'you think you're going?"

"Out." Steve stopped on the drive and turned back towards his father. "And she's got another man. He's the chef of the restaurant she works in."

*

For days Brian simmered. Steve's parting comment had left him standing in the kitchen speechless. It hadn't occurred to him Alison might have a lover. She'd seemed so centred on the house and garden; even when she'd worked, her motivation had been to earn money for the family. Until she started work at Le Pont. When Brian looked back, it became clear Alison's behaviour had changed over the last few months; she'd become more confident and ready to argue her case. He'd assumed she felt being the breadwinner gave her more power. But perhaps there was a different reason. Another man.

Brian hadn't been faithful to Alison. She'd taken so long to recover from the still birth of their second little boy, he'd been tempted to look elsewhere and found Tammy. He wasn't proud of that. More recently, as the strains in his marriage had grown, he'd met Carrie and would have welcomed a relationship with her. But she'd made it clear she wasn't interested. He realised that, if he could fancy other women, Alison could feel that way about other men. The idea of Alison in bed with another man sickened him. Although he tried to stop himself, he imagined a strange man humping her.

To clear his head, he walked out into the dark garden. The evening was growing cold and stars were emerging between tattered cloud banks; a barn owl floated from the direction of the church steeple and vanished. He told himself there was no evidence Alison was unfaithful, beyond the words Steve had flung. Maybe the accusation had been his way of hurting his father. That was likely, as he and Steve niggled and chafed against each other until they were both raw. But Alison had the opportunity, while she was at Le Pont, to mess about with another man. She rarely returned home during the afternoon break. Plenty of time for sex.

Half an hour had passed before Brian returned to the house, determined to know the truth. He thought of hanging around at Le Pont, talking to people, waiting until Alison emerged and confronting her. That would have to wait until he could persuade a neighbour to give him a lift to Caillac. Beside, he knew nothing about the chef Steve had talked about and didn't fancy a row with a man who had a kitchen full of knives. While Alison was at work, Brian tried looking through drawers. In amongst her clothes and a few pieces of costume jewellery, there were letters to friends back in England. Leafing through them made him feel uncomfortable and produced nothing incriminating. He wondered about some smart new underclothes, but they didn't count as evidence.

On Sunday, Brian got up late and had breakfast on his own, adding a glass or two of Armagnac. He was glad Steve had already taken a pair of binoculars and vanished. However, that left him alone with Alison. He watched her for any sign of unusual behaviour, and agreed to go shopping, because it gave him the opportunity to get out of St Thomas. And keep an eye on her.

Brian didn't much like supermarkets, as he still had a romantic image of France as a country of small shops and open markets. He had to admit the Intermarché was more convenient but it had the same glossy anonymity as the shops back in England. They drove in silence to the square block in an out-of-town estate and took a trolley. There was always a flurry before the supermarket closed at Sunday lunchtime and they had to wait behind several other shoppers filing through the doors. The fluorescent lights of the supermarket made him blink after the cool grey sky outside.

He crossed to the aisles devoted to wine, arranged in sections, each labelled with a region of France. "We could do with more wine."

"We can't afford it," said Alison and turned away.

Brian paused at a bin of cheap red wine and picked out two bottles. "We've always bought wine. It's cheap enough here."

"We've got to cut down. And you're drinking too much anyway."

A man squeezed past, wheeling his trolley towards the racks of Bordeaux wine.

"I bet you buy cosmetics and stuff for yourself." Brian stowed the bottles of wine in the trolley.

Alison steered it to the racks of soft drinks and chose one of the cheapest bottles of fruit drink.

Brian complained. "You're getting obsessed with money."

"You know why."

As they continued round the supermarket and queued at the

check out, his mind rehearsed his familiar arguments with Alison about their debts, and the question of selling the house. His grievances against her swirled, coalesced and took on the form of the chef at Le Pont. Although he'd no idea what this man was like: short or tall, fat or thin, Brian hated him. He grew determined to challenge Alison.

At the check out a plump girl assistant waited as Brian piled the shopping on the belt. Alison took out her debit card.

The girl looked at the card reader. "It's not working."

Brian took out his own card and pushed it into the slot.

"Perhaps it's the machine," said the girl, pushing her light brown hair from her face and bending over the card reader.

Alison shook her head and fumbled in her purse. "If I leave the washing powder out, I should have enough cash." She took the big packet of powder and the two bottles of wine out of the trolley and placed them beside the till.

The girl stared at her before cancelling the transaction and starting again.

"You might have left the wine," said Brian.

Clouds were pressing down on the shops opposite, as he pushed the trolley into the car park and threaded his way between the lines of cars. The wind was rising, catching plastic bags and wrapping them round the wheels of trolleys parked in bays.

"I told you we were in trouble," said Alison. "I won't be able to buy anything else until I get paid."

Brian stopped the trolley close to the car. The idea of the chef paying her sparked in his mind. "So at least he pays you."

"Of course I get paid. I'd hardly work there without."

A big black car drew up in the next bay and a small woman

stepped out, opened the boot and took out a shopping bag.

After letting her pass, Brian turned on Alison. "Wouldn't you? I'd heard there was more between you and that chef. What's his name?"

"What do you mean?"

"Are you having it off with him?"

As she took a few steps away from him, he fancied she went a shade paler."What on earth makes you think that?"

"Steve said."

She turned her face away, opened the car boot and lifted in a bag of shopping.

"I want an answer," he said, moving closer.

"I'm not talking to you." She loaded another bag of shopping in the boot.

He gasped. If she'd denied the accusation outright, he might have concluded Steve had made the story up. But she was just playing for time. "You slut. You fucking slut."

She rounded on him. "Don't you call me a slut. As if you haven't had other women. What about Carrie?"

"Carrie's just a friend. I've never done more than talk to her. It's a completely different thing. Or don't you understand the fucking difference?"

Two young men glanced at them as they walked past and climbed into a white van parked in a nearby space. Brian didn't care what they thought as he faced his wife.

"But there have been other women, haven't there?" said Alison. "When Steve was little."

"Don't change the subject. I want to know if you're fucking

that man or not?"

"Look at yourself. You're drunk half the time." Her face was flushed.

The vein in his neck was throbbing again. "You're a fucking two-faced bitch. You've been lecturing me on being sensible, paying our debts and all that. Making out you're somehow better than me. And all the time you're fucking some other man. That's why you're talking of leaving, isn't it? You want to be with that fucking French bastard."

"No, it's you. You're useless and irresponsible. Most women would have left ages ago."

He lurched towards her, let fly with his clenched fist and hit her hard on the ear. She tumbled against the lid of the car boot, slumped in a limp heap on the concrete and lay with blood flowing from a cut on her head.

Chapter 24

Steve had left the house straight after breakfast and climbed the hill, with the idea of watching deer. The air was cold and damp, covering twigs and cobwebs with skeins of dewdrops. He waited with camera, sketch pad and pencil case at the edge of a field surrounded by woods and high fences. The deer grazed, or stood poised on their long legs before disappearing into trees. Steve stayed crouching in the bushes, with his anorak zipped and his hood up. He took photos and tried to draw. It was impossible with his gloves on, so his hands were clumsy with cold by the time he finished, but he'd covered several pages with sketches. When he reached home, he was surprised his parents weren't back from shopping. They must have gone on elsewhere. He settled in his room to work on his rough sketches but, by lunchtime, he was beginning to wonder what had happened. Maybe they'd had a row. That wouldn't be surprising.

There was a knock on the door. Two gendarmes in navy uniforms stood there: a young woman whose hair was escaping from her cap, and a stout middle-aged man.

"Can we come in?" asked the man.

"I haven't done anything," Steve said as they edged into the kitchen.

The young woman shook her head. " You're not in trouble. We came to talk about your parents."

"They're not here."

The man was unthreatening, with his silver hair and round face, but made Steve nervous by walking round the kitchen inspecting the cooker and knife block. It looked as if he was searching for evidence of a crime. The young woman sat on one of the kitchen chairs, and took a notebook out of a pocket in her uniform.

"What's going on?" asked Steve, as he sat opposite her.

The man stopped exploring the kitchen and turned to face him. "Did your parents go to the Intermarché in Caillac this morning?"

"Maman said they were going shopping. I went out before they left," Steve said.

"But they haven't returned?"

"No. Look, has something happened?" His voice rose.

"We think there was an argument between your parents in the car park of the Intermarché," said the woman officer. "I'm afraid your mother was hurt. "

"What?"

The young woman reached across the table and put her hand on his arm. "Don't worry too much. They've taken her to the hospital at Castelnau. She was knocked unconscious but she's going to be all right."

Steve rose and drove his hands hard onto the table. He wished he'd been there, so he could have stopped Dad hurting Mum, although he might have killed Dad if he'd had the chance. He wouldn't have meant to but he got so angry. Knowing the two gendarmes were watching his reaction, he said nothing. Suddenly, his mind filled with a picture. He'd stood in the kitchen doorway and shouted at Dad that Mum had a lover. Perhaps this violence was his fault. Steve sat down again and lowered his face, as anger yielded to a confusion of guilt and distress. "Can I see Maman?"

"We'll take you to the hospital," the young woman said.

"What have you done with my Papa?"

"He's in custody at the moment," said the man.

Steve grabbed his anorak, his phone and some money and sat in the back of the gendarmes' car. When he was a child, he might have enjoyed a ride in a police car. Today he took little interest, as the gendarmes drove down the hill and across the plain alongside the Lot, occasionally responding to messages on the radio. Everything seemed unreal.

They drove through part of Castelnau unfamiliar to Steve. The first he saw of the hospital was a grand old building like a church with a dome, but the police car turned aside and parked by a collection of modern blocks. The gendarmes left their car near the entrance, walked with him between big sliding doors and stopped at a reception desk. A middle aged woman with permed hair looked Steve up and down with some disapproval. He hadn't realised his anorak and trousers were still stained with green and covered with bits of twig.

Having thanked the gendarmes, Steve found his way along corridors and up stairs. He stopped, uncertain, at the door of the ward to which he'd been directed. In the nearest bed an old woman lay draped in tubes. At last, he saw his mother in a bed near the window and hurried over. The area over her left eye was covered with a dressing and she looked pale.

Steve sat on a plastic chair by his mother's bed and placed his hand on hers.

She gazed at him, as if perplexed by his concern. "Are you all right, Steve?"

"I'm sorry Mum," he said, his voice wavering.

"What are you sorry about?"

"I told Dad about you and Nathalie's father. I didn't mean to. I just got so angry with him."

His mother jerked upright, but then sank back into the pillows, her mouth twisting with pain. "Where's Dad?"

"The gendarmes have got him."

The door opened and two men in blue overalls pushed a bed into the room, manoeuvring it into the opposite corner. Only a tuft of hair was visible above blankets, but a woman moaned.

"What happened?" asked Mum. "All I remember is going shopping."

"The gendarmes didn't really say, but I reckoned Dad hit you." Steve wrapped his hand around her long fingers. "I hope you're going to be all right."

She tried to smile but her lips quivered. "Don't worry about me."

A nurse in a neat white uniform entered the room, pushing a rattling trolley and stopped by Mum's bed. She was plump, with shadows under her eyes.

"I'm going to check Madame Delaney's dressing," she said. "Can you wait outside?"

"I'll be back," said Steve, as the nurse drew a green and white curtain round the bed.

*

On leaving the ward, Steve went in search of something to eat. He was starving. Having found a café on the ground floor, he bought a filled baguette and a Coca Cola. At one plastic table, several elderly people sat talking quietly and, at another, a woman comforted a baby, while a small girl drank out of a straw. It occurred to Steve he'd no way of getting home. He could have come on his scooter, but he hadn't thought of that when the gendarmes arrived. If he couldn't scrounge a lift from someone, he'd have to look for a bus to Caillac or hitch hike. He resigned himself to a long wait, but the events of the last few days clamoured in his mind. Sometimes he felt responsible for Dad hitting Mum; at other times he resented being drawn into a row that was not his concern. He took out his mobile phone and rang Nathalie. She understood these things better than he did. Beside, her father might want to know what had happened to his mother.

As time passed, he grew bored of sitting with his mother and wandering round the hospital. The glimpses of people attached to machines or swaddled in blankets made him uncomfortable. He strolled outside and found a park with a manicured lawn outside the old hospital building. However, the flower beds didn't interest him much and the rain that had threatened all day was beginning to fall.

As he walked back into the ward, Steve saw a dark-haired man with a Roman nose sitting at his mother's bedside, holding her hand. He was dressed in jeans and a dark green sweatshirt. A bunch of pink roses stood in a vase on her bedside cupboard. Steve remembered the mushroom-picking trip at the Ricaud's, and recognised François. He stopped, embarrassed.

Mum gestured for him to join her and François stood up.

"I'd better go, " Steve said.

"No, don't. Do you know François?"

Steve nodded.

François smiled and offered his hand. "We've met. Thank you for telling Nathalie what happened."

Steve solemnly shook hands.

The nurse who had spoken to his mother earlier entered the

ward and drew the curtains round the elderly woman's bed. There was quiet conversation and a groan.

François sat on the edge of Mum's bed and took her hand. "I hope we can get you out of here soon."

"They said I might be able to go home tomorrow If I have a home..." Mum hesitated.

Steve stood and felt in the way. From the glances his mother and François exchanged, Steve guessed they were wary of saying too much in front of him. He decided to show he could behave like an adult. "I know what's going on."

François nodded. "I'll talk to Yvonne Mathieu about those rooms over her shop. I'm sure she'd let you have them."

"What about you, Steve?" asked Mum.

Steve was dreading meeting his Dad again. It was hard to imagine talking to him normally, and any conversation might turn violent. But he didn't want to look as if he was afraid. "I'll be all right until Papa turns up. If anything happens, I'll get out of there, as long as I've got my scooter."

The nurse crossed over to his mother's bed. "I don't think you should stay too long," she said to the visitors. "Madame Delaney needs to rest."

François rose. "I'll be back tomorrow."

"Can you give me a lift home?" asked Steve.

François nodded. "Sure."

*

As it was dark and wet by the time Steve left the hospital with François, they hurried across the car park to a small, white van.

"Did the gendarmes say what they are going to do with your father?" asked François.

Steve shook his head. "They only said Maman was in hospital and they'd arrested Papa."

He was reluctant to say more and sat silent in the passenger seat, trying to trace their journey home by recognising villages and junctions with street lamps. He didn't want François to see him upset, but clenched his hand on the door handle. The van was scruffy in a way Steve understood: full of empty plastic crates, sacks and string. François drove the local roads with speed and confidence.

"Do you know where we live?" Steve asked, as the van followed the main road along the valley.

François smiled. "I've known these roads since I was your age."

He drove up the hill to St Thomas and parked on the triangle of grass behind the church. The village was silent and the house stood ghostly white in light from a nearby street lamp. The family's old Citroen was parked on the drive.

"Dad's home." Steve stood uncertain on the grass.

François came to join him. "Are you afraid he might hit you?"

"I might hit him," said Steve, clenching his hands.

François shook his head. "We don't want violence. I'll come with you."

Steve would never have admitted it but he found François's presence reassuring, as they walked across the road and down the drive to the kitchen door. Brian was sitting at the table with his head in his hands and a bottle of Armagnac at his side.

He raised his head and looked at Steve and François standing in the doorway. "Who's that?"

"I've been to see Mum," said Steve. "This is Monsieur Allombert. He's brought me home."

Brian rose, his eyes and skin red. "Are you Alison's fancy man? Get out of here before I throw you out."

"I have come here to make sure your son is safe," said François in careful English.

"It's all your fault, you wanker," said Brian, taking a few steps towards François.

He folded his arms but remained in the doorway. "You have done a bad thing. You have hit your wife. It would be another bad thing to hit your son."

Brian stopped and, for a long moment, the two men glared at each other. Steve moved closer to François, who looked calm and poised, standing with his feet a little apart. Dad was bleary eyed and unsteady, one hand on the kitchen table.

"Alison is unhappy because you drink too much and you do not pay your debts," said François. "She works but you do nothing. Already she wanted to leave you."

"How dare you say that?"

"I will leave. But if I hear that there is more violence, I will call the gendarmes and you will be in prison for a long time." François turned to Steve. " Phone me if there are problems."

François walked away, his footsteps crunching on the drive. Steve shut the door behind François and faced his father, wondering what to say. With his mother in hospital and Dad looking on the verge of collapse, it would be stupid to say anything to cause further violence, but ordinary conversation felt impossible. In the end, Steve opted for safety. "I think Mum's going to be all right. And I want something to eat."

Chapter 25

Monday afternoon was well advanced by the time Alison and François arrived outside Le Pont. François parked his van behind the restaurant and slipped his arm round Alison's waist as they walked to the rear of Yvonne Mathieu's flower shop. The little patio garden was empty, the bright summer flowers long gone. François knocked on the door of the small extension, where Alison had seen Yvonne taking in deliveries of flowers and plants. Although Alison had often chatted to Yvonne and regarded her as a friendly soul, she wondered how much to tell her. It would grieve her if lurid versions of the story circulated round the neighbourhood. In any case, she was still hazy about what had happened in the car park. All she knew was Brian had knocked her out and her marriage was over.

She'd spent the morning in the hospital. Although she had combed her hair and washed, she still felt dirty and dishevelled, because her only clothes were the trousers and blood-stained blue jersey she'd worn on that disastrous shopping trip. The cut on her forehead had been stitched and covered with a dressing but her head ached with every movement she made.

Half way through the morning, she'd decided to ensure she could still walk. She'd ambled out of the ward and along the corridor, before stopping at a window, from which she could see a car park and an expanse of neat lawn with flower beds. Soon afterwards, the doctor had checked the cut and said she was well enough to leave, but it had been another hour before François arrived to take her back to Caillac. She'd wondered what kept him, as Monday was one of the days when the restaurant was closed. Doubtless he was busy and, now they were together, he was clearly concerned about her. But perhaps he could have been quicker.

Yvonne opened the door and wiped her hands on the striped apron she wore over her skirt and cardigan. She was short and rounded, with hair which was neatly permed, although grey roots peeped out beneath the brown. The lines round her eyes and mouth gave the impression of good humour.

"Excuse me. I've been potting some plants," she said, embracing Alison.

As they stepped inside, Yvonne gestured at a storeroom to the left. Flowers filled rows of buckets, while bags of compost, pots and wicker baskets were stacked in the far corner.

"I'm starting to prepare for Christmas already. I've just had a delivery of baubles for Christmas wreaths. It gets earlier each year."

Alison nodded, wondering how she would spend Christmas. The sort of family Christmases she remembered from her childhood were out of the question. Despite her father's strict views on some subjects, Christmas had been celebrated in the traditional way, with a tree and crackers, presents and turkey. This year Brian would be missing, but she hoped Steve and François would be there.

Alison and François followed Yvonne up a flight of stone stairs to the shop, then carpeted stairs to the flat. As Yvonne opened the door, Alison noticed a musty smell.

"It's been empty for years," said Yvonne. "I left here after I had my children, but my daughter used it for a while. I gave it a quick clean when I knew you were coming but.."

"Don't worry," said Alison, aware that her sudden arrival had given Yvonne work.

While Alison and François walked round the flat, Yvonne pointed to useful cupboards and talked about the years she'd spent there. The living room was furnished with two armchairs, which must have originally had a green and cream pattern, although the fabric was now so threadbare it was difficult to make out lines and leaves. The white painted plaster was peeling in places and there were grey patches of damp round the windows. In the main bedroom, Alison looked out of the window with François at her side. The surface of the river, so placid in the summer, was rising into crests, and the white boats had moved on for the winter. The old warehouse on the far bank looked grey and dilapidated. Alison felt the flat was good enough for now and could be improved with some paint and a few ornaments, but it wasn't home. With a shock, she realised the house in St Thomas wasn't home either. Not any longer.

Of course what mattered was not the place you lived in but the people you shared it with. Alison drew a finger over the window, leaving a line in dust, while she wondered about Steve. Would he want to come and join her here? When François had told her about the confrontation in St Thomas, she'd grasped his hand tight in concern about Steve. Was he safe? Could he stay in the house with Brian? She imagined rows, hurled insults, even violence. When she'd tried ringing Steve's mobile, there was no reply, which made her more nervous. Although he wasn't meant to switch it on at school, she wasn't sure if he had gone. François had reassured her, saying he thought Steve an intelligent young man, well able to look after himself. Although Alison knew that was true, she still worried and hoped he'd come to join her here.

Even given the modest rent Yvonne proposed, it would be a stretch to afford a two bedroom flat. She could only manage if she gave up the car and, even so, the cost wouldn't be justified if it was only for herself. The move only made sense if Steve came too. When François met her gaze but said nothing, she knew she shouldn't depend on his opinion, as she had Brian's. It was her decision.

Alison was jerked out of her reflection when Yvonne moved a little dish on the window sill. She swallowed. "I'd be glad to have it."

"I want to make sure you're safe," said François. "But it would be good if you could get back to work when you feel well enough."

"I'll be all right by tomorrow. But I need to go back to St Thomas for some things. I've got nothing at the moment."

François frowned. "You may have to wait until Sunday. I'll be busy until then."

Alison remembered the remark Nathalie had made soon after they first met – for François, his restaurant always came first. Maybe she was right. For the first time Alison felt she could understand the reasons for Simone's unhappiness. It would be difficult to be married to a man who was so busy working he could never find time to meet his wife's needs.

Once Alison had agreed terms with Yvonne, they walked down the stairs and stood chatting outside the door for a while. Alison had her back to Le Pont but she noticed the voices. Two young people stood on the patio, empty since the tables had been stored away for the winter. Nathalie and Steve. His scooter was parked near the wall, with her school bag and his rucksack dumped beside it.

"Steve!" Alison hurried over to her son. "Have you come to stay?"

"Reckon. I can't live with Dad. We'd be rowing all the time and, if he thumped me, I might kill him."

Alison hugged him. "I'm so glad to have you here."

***

Next Sunday evening, Brian was alone in the house in St Thomas. He sat on the sofa in the living room, with a cigarette in his hand. Unopened letters littered the coffee table in front of him, alongside an ashtray, a glass and an empty bottle of Armagnac. The waste-paper basket next to the sofa was full of flyers from local shops. He'd been brooding since Alison and that bastard of a chef turned up in the morning and insisted that Alison took her possessions. As she emptied out drawers it became clear she had no intention of returning home. Until then, Brian thought she and Steve might forgive him for the unfortunate incident in the car park. He hadn't meant to hurt her. She'd provoked and driven him past his breaking point.

Brian followed her from room to room as she packed boxes. He accepted she needed clothes but argued about family photographs. They were part of his history. When she collected Steve's artwork, as well as his clothes and books, she stripped his room of its familiar personality. Brian was reluctant to argue with François, who could convey authority by standing in a doorway and watching. However, Brian had refused to relinquish the car, despite the driving ban, as he would be stuck in St Thomas without it. François pointed out Brian had to face the more serious charge of wounding Alison. That might land him in prison. Helpless and humiliated, Brian watched them drive away.

He missed his wife and son more than he could have imagined. Wherever he went in the house, he looked for them. Until things started going wrong, Alison had brought warmth and comfort, not just by cooking and cleaning but also by her presence. Although Steve could be annoying, he'd filled the house with life and, in the last year, his school work and drawings had given Brian a cause for pride. Without them, the house became dreary and depressing.

The quiet he once found soothing became oppressive. His footsteps echoed on the quarry tiles; spiders span webs across doorways and between chair legs. Outside, winter wind and rain kept the villagers he knew indoors. He had lost so much.

There had been other times in his life when he'd felt defeated, including the row with his boss at the Greenaway Agency and the collapse of his bookshop. But he'd never given up hope and, after thought, he'd come up with alternatives. Now he faced despair. With Alison and Steve gone there wasn't much motivation for rebuilding. Although he could try to visit Carrie, he couldn't imagine telling her his sorry tale. What would she think of him? When he'd last knocked on her door, she'd almost closed it in his face. And there was his parlous financial position to worry about. He'd left the latest letters from banks unopened, because he knew they'd be demands for payments of debt he couldn't meet. There would be no money coming in unless he pleaded with Alison. Although he made a case for the car, he couldn't afford to run it. In a few weeks time he might be either in prison or destitute. He padded into the kitchen and scanned the shelves where the wine was kept. There weren't many bottles left but he returned with some cheap local brandy, poured himself a glass, sat down and lit a cigarette.

He wanted to dismiss the niggling worry this mess was his fault. François had suggested it was. Although Brian didn't rate the chef's opinion, the words kept returning to his mind, like some bad tune. He looked at the glass of brandy and held it under the light, watching the liquid glow and move. Of course he liked a drink, a lot of men did and maybe a pleasure had turned into a habit. But that didn't give Alison the right to fuck another man. As for working, he'd tried. He'd come up with several ideas to make money after that bastard of a mayor said 'non' to their renovation project. Maybe they hadn't worked, but that wasn't his fault, was it? Could he have done better? Maybe his decisions had been unwise. He hadn't realised how difficult it would be to renovate the barn and establish a *chambre d'hôte.* And his attempts to trade antiques suggested it might take years to establish a business. As Brian stubbed his cigarette out into a saucer, his hand trembled.

He poured himself one glass after another. A man had to take risks to achieve anything. Everybody was against him – first the mayor, now Alison and that chef. It wasn't fair. Lots of men would have acted as he did, finding his wife fucking another man. He shouldn't let the bastards get him down. Maybe, if he worked as hard as he knew how, he could still get out of this mess. The gendarmes had believed him when he said he hadn't meant to hurt Alison, so maybe the tribunal would let him off with a fine. He'd cut down his drinking and get a job. There must be something he could do, like return to writing the novel he'd started. If he finished maybe someone would publish it. He could write without even leaving the house.

Realising he hadn't eaten since breakfast Brian got up, swaying and knocked the ashtray and a slew of post off the table. In the kitchen, he found the fridge empty apart from a stale baguette and a packet of sausages. He poured oil into a frying pan, threw the sausages in and listened to them sizzle. For a moment, he thought of Alison and that chef sitting down to a fancy French meal. They could keep it, as sausages would do for him. Brian tipped them onto a plate, found a knife and fork and sat down to eat. Having finished eating, he sat at the kitchen table, letting his eyelids droop. He had a vague impression there was a smell of smoke from somewhere, but paid no attention. What he needed at the moment was to stop worrying and leave his attempts to sort his life out to another day.

Chapter 26

When Alison's mobile phone rang, she didn't at first recognise the number and answered in an off-hand tone.

Valérie Couzineau's voice quavered with alarm. "Alison, I'm very sorry. There's bad news."

"What's happened? Is it Brian?" Her mind galloped – a road accident, perhaps.

"Your house is on fire. We've called the *sapeurs pompiers* but ..."

"Where's Brian?"

"I don't know. We're not sure if he was..."

"I'll come straight away."

Yvonne Mathieu rose from her armchair. "Is there something wrong? Do you need a lift?"

Before the phone rang, they had been sitting in the living room of Alison's flat talking about life with teenagers. There were still boxes full of personal possessions to unpack but Alison had abandoned the task to chat to Yvonne. She accepted the offer of a lift with genuine gratitude and grabbed a coat. Then hesitated. What to tell Steve? He had shut himself in his bedroom, saying he would put away his own clothes. When she opened his door, clothes were strewn across the floor, but he was sitting on the bed, with his sketch pad and a set of paints on a little table.

"I'm going out for a while," she said, trying to keep her voice level. "Can you get yourself something to eat?"

He put down his paint brush. "Is something up?"

She tried to play down the seriousness of the problem. "Valérie said there's been a fire in our house. I don't know if there's much damage. I want to go and see for myself."

"Can I come?"

"You'd better not. I don't suppose the firemen want lots of people around."

He stared at her for a moment, then shrugged and turned back to his drawing.

Yvonne's small Peugeot rattled and bounced along minor roads in the dark, until they rounded a bend and Alison saw a glow over St Thomas. She grasped the car door handle. As they approached the top of the hill, a group of firemen in high visibility jackets and helmets stopped them. Yvonne parked the car at the edge of a plum orchard and Alison ran. Two fire engines stood on the triangle of grass behind the church and a tangle of hoses stretched across the road, while firemen with breathing apparatus trained high pressure jets of water at smoke and flames swirling round the house. Their car was standing on the drive. What had happened to Brian? Was he in that chaos? If so, his chances were slim.

Alison hurried between the fire engines, stepping over hoses, until she found a burly man with a radio who appeared to be in charge.

"Please. I'm afraid my husband's in there."

"We'll do everything we can but you must move back." He laid a gloved hand on her shoulder and led her away from the fire.

Alison stumbled away and met Yvonne, who took her arm and stood beside her, silent for once. Although smoke filled Alison's lungs and heat scorched her face, she watched transfixed, as the fire eddied around windows and leapt towards the roof.

Valérie Couzineau appeared from behind a fire engine, with her coat clasped round her. "Come to our house. There's nothing you can do here. It would be better to get away from the smoke."

Alison followed Valérie and Yvonne to the Couzineau's house, where Albert met her at the door. Although his blue eyes met hers for a long moment he said nothing.

"I'm glad you could come," Valèrie said. "I didn't know where you were."

Alison wondered if Valérie knew she'd left Brian. But she wasn't going to explain, as it seemed irrelevant now. For a while they sat round the kitchen table, not speaking much while Valérie filled glasses with brandy. Alison was half aware of shouts from the firemen and the clock ticking in the kitchen.

As she sat, an image of former contentment formed in her mind. In the summer after they arrived in France, the essential repair work to the house had been completed and they looked forward to the renovation of the barns. She and Brian had sat at a table on the lawn, under the shade of the ragged pine tree, eating lunch of bread and cheese with red wine. Although Brian had always liked wine, it wasn't then a problem. He was cheerful, talking about their lives together since they had met: the places they had been and the good fortune they had shared when they arrived in St Thomas and found the house of their dreams. She had sat contemplating a future where they could be comfortable and happy together.

A knock at the door made her look round. Valérie left the room and returned with the chief fireman. He'd taken off his helmet, revealing brown hair above a face grey with soot.

"Madame Delaney?"

She nodded.

"I'm very sorry. My men brought a man out. The paramedics tried but he didn't respond. It was the smoke."

Yvonne rose and put her arm around Alison.

She gazed at the fireman as if she didn't understand, then realised there was no need for the men to take further risks. "There's two canisters of propane in the cellar."

He nodded, said something on a radio and hurried out of the house.

Some instinct made Alison follow him and pick her way between fire engines until she found the ambulance. It was parked on the road not far from their house, gaudy in white, yellow and red. As if expecting Brian to appear, she watched paramedics loading equipment through the rear doors. The men were taking their time.

A few minutes later a sudden explosion shook the village and a blossom of red flame and dark smoke opened against the night sky. The Couzineaus and Yvonne hurried across the road and stood with Alison. Walls and roofs disappeared as flames and smoke rose, roaring and throwing up shreds of paper and wood. In the confusion, Alison saw a youth pushing a scooter across the grass in her direction.

"Steve! What are you doing here? I thought I told you to stay at home."

He waved at the mass of smoke and flame."Dad?"

*

Cloud lay thick over St Thomas, marooning the village on an island, with houses and plum orchards blurring and disappearing. Alison stood, waiting for the hearse, with Steve beside her, hunched in a black anorak and looking at the road at his feet. Tim and Helen had flown over as soon as they could, bringing her mother. Alison was glad of their reassuring presence, but Daphne looked shrivelled and cold in her black coat. The group stood in front of a row of traffic cones blocking the drive to the house. The ruins of the house.

Alison had returned two days after the fire and seen the extent of the damage. The roof had collapsed into a heap of charred wood and broken tiles and, although most of the limestone walls were still standing, stones had fallen round the crack they had mended. In the rubble, drenched in water from the firemen's hoses, she'd spotted remnants of possessions. The base of the writer's chair protruded from a pile of tiles and, not far away, lay one of Brian's shoes. She'd turned away.

Today, she stood facing the road. She wasn't sure how she'd made it to this day. The whole period since Brian's death seemed unreal. It seemed she was standing somewhere apart, looking at herself acting rationally: making phone calls, speaking to people, filling in forms. Yet the part that coped didn't seem her real self. That was stunned. Fortunately, she'd been spared the task of identifying Brian's body and the police had decided the circumstances of his death weren't suspicious. She had phoned Tim and François, but was surprised to find everyone in the village and neighbourhood knew. There were offers of help from strangers. She thought the Mayor had been organising help – something Brian wouldn't have believed.

As the hearse appeared round the corner, Steve took Alison's hand. It was a long while since her son had offered such a gesture and she squeezed his fingers. He must be as confused inside as she was, if not more. Although he wasn't saying so, there was enough fellow feeling between them for her to understand. At least they had each other. The hearse slowed as it reached the drive. On the pine coffin lay a spray of white chrysanthemums and a simple wreath, which her mother had given.

The cost of the funeral had worried Alison. She couldn't afford even the simplest cremation and she wasn't sure what sort of funeral Brian would have chosen. When his father died, they'd ruled out a Catholic funeral, as Eddie had lost touch with the faith of his childhood. They'd compromised with an address by an Anglican clergyman, which was so bland as to be meaningless. Brian was rude about it afterwards. He had little time for religion. Alison had considered getting his body cremated, until she realised the nearest crematorium was on the road to Bordeaux. Although it would cost more to arrange a burial and she needed to buy a concession in the cemetery, some instinct insisted Brian's body should stay in the village they'd come to love. It was a relief when Tim told her to stop worrying about the cost, as he'd pay for the funeral.

Alison watched the hearse pass, then stepped out into the road. Steve walked on her left, still holding her hand, while Tim, Helen and Daphne followed at a slow pace. The Couzineaus crossed the road from their house, dressed in formal black, Valérie leaning on her stick. The hearse passed the Mairie, the remaining houses in the village and a leafless plum orchard, before turning right at the edge of a wood belonging to the château. The air was so damp water droplets fringed every twig and dripped onto the road as they passed.

When they reached the village cemetery, the hearse stopped and one of the bearers opened the gate. Alison stood, uncertain. Everywhere she looked there were family monuments: chambers of stone topped with engraved plaques. By the little brass fences surrounding the tombs, mourners had left plastic flowers and drooping bunches of real ones. Brian would have a plain slab. At last, the bearers slid the coffin from the hearse and carried it into the cemetery. Tim laid a hand on her arm and together they followed the bearers between the graves to an empty space. A simple trench. A grave digger stood nearby, wearing plain, dark clothes and holding a spade.

The undertakers had offered Alison the chance of a quiet room near their offices in Castelnau, where they could hold their own tribute to Brian. She'd been perplexed. What form would such a tribute take? After everything that had happened, it wouldn't be honest to give Brian a glowing eulogy. But he'd been such an important part of her life, she couldn't imagine burying him without some farewell. But what? It seemed unlikely anyone except family and a few neighbours would want to pay their respects. Brian had become so isolated. Everyone had deserted him. In the end she agreed to dispense with the room and arrange for Tim to say a few words in the cemetery. It felt inadequate but what else could they do? The circumstances were so difficult.

The bearers laid the coffin gently on a plastic sheet on the grass, moved the wreaths to one side and the group arranged itself round the grave. Tim straightened his dark tie and stepped forward.

"I wanted to say a few words of farewell to Brian Delaney. I knew him as the husband of my sister Alison and father to Steven but he had played many roles in his life. His death came so suddenly it was a great shock to us all – particularly Alison and Steve. I, for one, want to offer them all the support and understanding I can."

As Tim stopped for a moment, Alison wrapped her arm round Steve, who was rubbing his eyes on the sleeve of his anorak.

"I think we should concentrate on remembering Brian's life – the things he did and tried to do. Brian was a man who always aspired to do more and be more than people expected of him."

Tim spoke of Brian's childhood in Croydon, his success in getting a degree in English from Kent University, and his work as a copywriter in London. When Tim talked about Brian's marriage to Alison, he smiled a little at his sister. Alison realised she'd left the photos of her wedding in the house. For some reason, even in this chaos, that mattered. She'd told everybody, including herself, she had no love left for Brian. Was that true?

Tim went on to describe how Brian tried to run a bookshop but, when that failed, returned to advertising and accepted the responsibility of being a husband and father. The Couzineaus were standing, awkward, by the grave. Alison was aware they wouldn't understand the words but could do nothing to help. Tim continued, explaining how Brian decided what he really wanted was to move to France, where he could run a *chambre d'hôte* and write a novel. "Although his dream never quite worked out, we shouldn't blame him for dreaming. His mistake was to risk the things he loved for his dream. We shouldn't be too hard on him, as most of us fall short of the things we could have been. We should remember Brian at his best. He was intelligent and witty and threw himself into his enterprises with enthusiasm. He loved and was loved. Although we are burying his body, his memory will remain in the hearts of those left behind. But now it is time to say goodbye."

Tim took a step back and nodded to the bearers. They lowered the coffin into the ground, the grave digger stepped forward and started shovelling the earth on top. For a long while, Alison stood staring at the earth until Helen took her arm and led her away. The clouds had parted, freeing uncertain light to fall on the fields descending beyond the cemetery fence. The little village of St Thomas nestled round its church, as it had for generations. Somewhere in the valley down below, a tractor was ploughing.

Chapter 27

When Alison returned to Le Pont at the beginning of December, François was considerate. He welcomed her with a hug and came to the sink to check on her more often than usual. There was time, because business was slow. Instead of rushing to deal with lunchtime service, the chefs loitered, chatting to each other and the waiting staff. Alison looked out of the window at the river lapping grey against its banks. No-one was strolling along the driveway, and the traffic on the bridge seemed desultory compared to summer, as if everything was closing down for winter. It was easy to hide her face in the steam from the sink and let her mind drift. She hadn't seen François since Brian's death and, if she was honest with herself, she hadn't thought of him much. But she'd had so many worries.

After the funeral, the family had gone to Le Pont for an evening meal, which proved awkward. Although François had served a splendid dinner, she hadn't eaten much. She'd told Helen she'd left Brian before the fire but refused to say more, as it was too painful to talk about the circumstances of his death. Steve had sat in silence, only responding in monosyllables to his grandmother's questions. Daphne had looked thin and frail, but sat erect and looked around in interest.

She had news. "You know I've decided to move to a flat near Bristol? At least I'll be close to Tim, if not you."

"I'm glad," Alison said, ignoring the hint of criticism that always underlay her mother's comments.

"There's sure to be money left after I sell the house. You can have some of it, if you like."

Alison shook her head. "I don't want to take anything you need. I'll manage."

Tim smiled, reassuring. "Don't worry. I'll make sure Mum has enough left."

"I'm not gaga yet either," Daphne said, in a sharp tone.

"Thank you, Mum. That would be so helpful." Alison got up, pushing back her chair and gave her mother a hug. The truth was a gift of money from the sale of her mother's house would make her own future easier.

The house in St Thomas would be rebuilt. When she'd rung the insurance company, she'd dreaded the girl who answered the phone would say the bill hadn't been paid. To her relief, payments were up to date. The new house would be sold to cover the debt to the bank but she didn't mind. The emotions associated with the place would stay with her forever, but they belonged to the old house. That was a pile of stones.

Her main worry had been Steve. He'd hardly spoken at all after his father's death and she'd been reluctant to leave him while he was so raw with grief and confusion. It was only after she'd met Nathalie outside Le Pont and begged her to talk to Steve, that he regained some of his normal equilibrium and returned to school. Now, he was saying he might join the fire brigade. She could understand his interest, after his father's death, but hoped he wasn't haunted by fire. Brian's death had cast a cloud over Steve's life as well as her own, changing the landscape like a volcanic eruption.

*

Once the last customers had left and the washing up was finished, she walked up to the flat with François, with his arm round her waist. The winter light on blue shutters and white sheets made the bedroom look cold, while the layer of dust on surfaces had grown, suggesting no-one had bothered to clean. After more than three weeks apart, she hoped their love making would rekindle their relationship. It was good to nuzzle François's neck and feel his hands caressing her breasts but, as she parted her thighs and he pushed himself into her, it felt dull, unsatisfying. Something was missing, because part of her mind was elsewhere.

After they had made love, she asked François if he was worried about the slow pace of business.

He raised himself from the bedclothes on one elbow. "We're going to be busy in the couple of weeks before Christmas. We've got lots of bookings. Then we get a chance of a rest."

"You must be looking forward to Christmas," she said, her head still on the pillow.

"Of course. Pierre is coming home. You'll have a chance to get to know him."

Alison sat up. She needed to make a decision. François had said he'd close Le Pont after Christmas for a thorough clean and wouldn't open again until March, as there wasn't enough business. That had given her a problem. "I've been offered a job. Georges Ricaud told me the company that buys his peaches want someone who can phone importers in England."

"You mean you're leaving Le Pont?"

"I can't afford to stop working until March."

"But we'll go on seeing each other, won't we?"

She hesitated. "It's been difficult. I can't forgive myself for what happened. Brian's death and everything."

As the numbness of the days after Brian's death began to ease, all sorts of regrets and worries had pressed in on her mind. It was easy to ask what would have happened if she hadn't met François, or they hadn't become lovers. Could she have saved Brian, or was he on a path to self-destruction?

"You said you didn't love Brian." François was frowning. "Have you changed your mind?"

Alison shook her head. "But twenty two years of marriage must mean something." At the dinner in Le Pont, Daphne had said outright Alison should never have married Brian. Alison disagreed. Although the end of her marriage was disastrous, there had been much shared experience and plenty of tenderness. And without Brian, there would be no Steve.

"I don't want to be jealous of a man who's died."

"It's not that." Alison hesitated, her emotions too confused to be expressed easily. "There are things I need to do, and at the same time I'm trying to get my thoughts straight in my mind. All that stuff is getting in the way of us."

François wrapped his arm round her and drew her towards him. "Can I help?"

"You don't have much time. And I feel I've become a nuisance to you." She lay her head on his shoulder, glad of the comfort and reassurance of his strength and was tempted to change her mind. But she wasn't convinced by the offer of help. It would be limited by the needs of the business. When she'd phoned him to scrounge some extra leave, he'd sounded grudging, although it shouldn't have been a problem, given the circumstances and the slack business in November.

" You know how busy I am. " He frowned.

She drew away from him. "I think it's coming to an end. Don't you?" She leaned out of the bed, picked her bra out of the pile of

227

clothes on the floor and put it on.

He stepped out of bed naked and started to dress. "It was good what we had. Perhaps give it some time..."

She nodded. He was right, it had been good to be in his arms, sometimes passionate and always comforting. But the passion was beginning to fade and she needed independence more than comfort. He hadn't been prepared to take risks for her, while she'd risked and lost a great deal for him. Of course, she'd gained as well. François had shown her she was still an attractive woman. She was taking more care over her appearance and walking differently: her head held high. More important, she'd learned she could rely on her own abilities and make her own decisions. She finished dressing and stood by the door ready to leave.

April 2010

Steve rode to St Thomas on his scooter, carrying a rucksack bulging with notebooks, a laptop and camera. He'd told his mother he was studying the garrigue vegetation typical of the limestone ridges and plateaux of the area. True, that fitted his degree programme at Toulouse University but there were better examples elsewhere. In fact, he still dreamt of his father, sawing logs under the barn roof, picking purple plums or, of course, sitting at the kitchen table with a bottle in his hand, his face red with too much drink. Steve could feel the sun on the back of his neck. The morning clouds were beginning to unravel, and the temperature was rising. Everything was growing: from pale bronze leaves on poplars to green lines stitched on hillsides by the plum orchards.

He came to a stop outside the house on the corner. For a moment, he could have believed it was the place he'd lived in for two and a half years. But it wasn't. The old house had gone and been replaced by a new one. The walls were still limestone white but his mother said they were only stone-faced, the rest being insulated blocks. The shutters were brown, but natural oak rather than the chocolate he remembered.

As he watched, a young boy burst out of the back door of the house, followed more slowly by a woman with a toddler. They were heading down into the garden. Even from the road, Steve could see the old fruit trees and a swing hanging from one of them. The plum trees had finished flowering, but the apples were covered with pink and white blossom. His mother would love to see them. Although she worked for a fruit exporter, she spent most of her time at a desk in Castelnau, a long way from the orchards.

When he'd arrived for Christmas, he'd promised to help Mum repaint the flat, which she described as 'dreary.' He'd splashed a lot of primrose coloured paint on walls, which brightened the place, and hung up one of his paintings of a deer. Mum had bought a television, having done without one since the fire, and they'd sat and watched it together. It was easy to imagine Dad sitting in one of the faded armchairs, passing caustic comments on the old films. He'd have said the story lines were clichéd, or the dialogue stilted. Steve didn't care. It was good to see his mother looking less strained, almost as if she was growing younger. The money from the sale of Gran's house had enabled her to pay off their remaining debts, but she became thoughtful if he asked her about Dad.

Remembering his real reason for visiting St Thomas, Steve rode up the narrow street, past the white church and one of the plum orchards, and turned right to the cemetery. Even here, spring had brought renewal, as the field sloping down into the valley was green with growing wheat, while wild orchids were flowering on the verge. He knew their name now: early spider orchids. In the past, he wouldn't have cared about flowers, but studying ecology had taught him every living thing was interconnected. Steve left his scooter by the stone wall and entered the cemetery. It didn't take him long to find his father's grave, as it was one of a few single slabs amongst family tombs. Here and there people had left flowers in vases at the base of a tomb: roses or white lilies. Steve hadn't brought flowers, as his Dad wouldn't have cared for them, only being interested in vegetables or fruit trees. Instead, he took out a framed photo of himself and his mother at Christmas and placed it on the slab. "I hope you're proud of me, Dad," he murmured. "I'm doing all right at uni." Then he took a step back.

People said he looked more like his Dad than Mum. Which was he more like in character: Dad, with his imagination, or Mum, always hard-working and reliable? Almost always. Her affair with François no longer troubled him. It would be good to believe he could take the best from both his parents and mix them together, in the way his mother made a cake, but Steve understood enough about genetics to know he couldn't make this choice. He would make the best of what he had.

He left the cemetery, mounted his scooter and rode through the quiet village, past the rebuilt house and down the hill. At the first bend in the road, he stopped and took his camera out of his rucksack. He took a photograph of the village with a plum orchard in the foreground, a huddle of houses and the white church. One for the record.

Acknowledgements

I am very grateful to Susannah Waters, my tutor on the Creative Writing Programme and Advanced Writing Workshops. Without her help, this novel would never have been finished. Also to my writing friends, particularly Lucy Corkhill, Christine Kilgour and Louise Roddon, for their encouragement and support.

I would also like to thank my husband Peter Neumann and our son Geoffrey for understanding my endeavour and aiding and abetting in a whole range of ways.

Made in the USA
Charleston, SC
30 October 2015